The Way Beauty Comes Apart

First Published in the US in 2025 by Ovunque Siamo Press
Ambler, Pennsylvania
www.ovunquesiamoweb.com/

Publisher's Cataloging-in-Publication Data
Names: Marrocco, Christina, author.
Title: The way beauty comes apart : a novel-in-stories / Christina Marrocco.
Description: Ambler, PA: Ovunque Siamo, 2025.
Identifiers: LCCN: 2025913391 | ISBN: 979-8-9862692-3-8 (print) | 979-8-9862692-4-5 (ebook)
Subjects: LCSH Wales--Fiction. | Wales--Social life and customs--Fiction. | Death--Fiction. | Women--Fiction. | Short stories. | BISAC FICTION / Cultural Heritage | FICTION / Literary | FICTION / Women
Classification: LCC PS3613 .A77 W39 2025 | DDC 813.6--dc23

This book is a work of fiction. Names, places, characters, businesses, organizations, and events are either a product of the author's imagination or used fictitiously. Any resemblance to actual persons, living or dead, events or locales, is entirely coincidental. This book is entirely the work of the author and developed solely using imagination, research, and years of work. There has been no Generative AI use in any aspect of this book, from invention to revision to editing. The author encourages readers to read real books written by real people and writers to write real books so that we may keep and strengthen humanity.

Epigraph couplet by Dic Jones with permission of the Estate of Dic Jones
Editing and project consultation by Alis Hawkins
Translations and project coaching by Brychan Jones
Book design by Adam Robinson, Good Book Developers
Publicity and marketing by Dan Klefstad
Cover design by Rob Dunbar, Dunbar Design LLC
Administrative and editorial project support by Karen Formanski, Conspire Creative

Praise for *The Way Beauty Comes Apart*

'A work of immense charm, of revelation and of deep empathy with the people of the past.'
—Alis Hawkins, author of the four-part *Teifi Valley Coroner Series*, *Bitter Remedy*, *The Skeleton Army*, and *The Hunters Club*

'Tragedy makes us appreciate life. But when Christina Marrocco lets the doomed speak their truth, we get a deeper insight into the fragility and fleeting beauty of existence. Her novel-in-stories, *The Way Beauty Comes Apart*, embraces the ill-fated, giving readers a master class in empathy. I mourn and celebrate each of them, and I'm sure you will too.'
—Dan Klefstad, long-time radio host and newscaster for National Public Radio and author of *Fiona's Guardians*

'This collection of beautifully wrought vignettes offers fascination, pathos, humour and perceptive pride in the small Welsh community. I invite you to discover how beauty comes apart: You won't regret it!'
—Chris Malone, blogger and author of the *# Glitch Trilogy*

'Award-winning novelist Christina Marrocco dispels the notion that the dead tell no tales. In the fictional village of Nefin, she raises its dead to captivate you with their secrets, their sorrows, their hard-scrabble, interconnected lives. Immersed in prose that is lush and atmospheric and mesmerizing, you are no armchair traveler looking in – you are there, you know the landscape and the language, its cadence as familiar as your own. Marrocco brings these villagers and their home to life so vividly that you turn the last page wishing she'd let you linger in Nefin a wee bit more.'

—Karen Tintori, *Unto the Daughters: The Legacy of an Honor Killing in a Sicilian Family*

'Christina Marrocco is an absolute master of the novel-in-stories. *The Way Beauty Comes Apart* gives voice to the Welsh dead. This novel resonates with George Saunders's *Lincoln in the Bardo* as well as Edgar Lee Masters's *Spoon River Anthology*, but unlike those works, Marrocco's characters know they are dead, and they meditate on their deaths but also their lives. They tell us about their beliefs, such as visitations from a God who doesn't save them; they recount their profound sorrows from losing their babies to cot death, which told from a different character's perspective reveals an ill-informed but well-intentioned attempt to quiet crying babies. They tell the reader of their longing to leave their provincial village and travel to the metropole of London but are denied the chance because they are the victim of unwanted male lust. They question the faith they were taught as they come to terms with human evolution and fossil evidence that belies a simplistic faith.

In every story, we are moved and edified by Marrocco's exquisite, compassionate imagination that allows us to place an ear to the ground and hear the voices of the long dead who, despite their isolation in rural North West Wales, are very much like us. Readers will be enraptured by the lyrical prose and the careful attention to world building that depicts an earlier era in a land steeped in folklore and fairytale enchantment while also on the cusp of modernity.'

—Kathleen Williams Renk, author of the award-winning *Vindicated: A Novel of Mary Shelley*, *The Rossetti Diaries* and *No Coward Soul Have I*

The Way Beauty Comes Apart

A Novel-in-Stories
Christina Marrocco

Ovunque Siamo Press
2025

Also by Christina Marrocco

Addio, Love Monster
BOOK OF THE YEAR
CHICAGO WRITERS ASSOCIATION, 2022

Introduction by Alis Hawkins

It was an odd email to receive as an editor. An American from Chicago—a published, award-winning novelist—who'd written a novel made up of linked short stories set in North West Wales, was looking for editorial input and advice on publishing in the UK, preferably Wales. It wasn't the first time I'd edited a manuscript by a non-UK author, but it was the first time I'd edited a collection of short stories. That gave me pause for thought, as did the question of what an American could possibly have to say about Wales that might be of interest to people here.

But when I'd read the manuscript Christina Marrocco sent me, I knew I had to work on this book. Because it seemed to me that, through a kind of ancestral, alchemical empathy, *The Way Beauty Comes Apart* had allowed the people of the fictional village of Nefin to speak the truth of their diverse lives in a small, close-knit community in North West Wales.

Christina and I worked together over a period of months to pick and hone the stories that best reflected the sense of entwined, interdependent lives that this book represents. In *How Beauty Comes Apart* working-class women who fall under the spell of revivalist Methodist preachers rub shoulders with young women who want nothing more than to escape the claustrophobic propriety of their village community for London's fashion world. An autodidact stone picker engages in philosophical conversation with a high-class shopkeeper-cum-travelling adventurer. A bad but charismatic man who dominates the banter in the local pub is pitted against women who watch over the community and, as women always have, ensure the safety of the next generation.

All this richness of social class and belonging and need for escape stems from the author's deep fascination and sense of connection with the area around Nefyn and Pwllheli. On several occasions, over from America, she has walked this area and has wandered among the graves of now moribund churches whose dead seemed to whisper to her, with the voice of her Welsh ancestors, 'We're still here'. Determined to tell their stories, she entered into an exercise in imagination that has produced something quite wonderful.

Sometimes, it takes an outsider to show us ourselves and then throw light on the lives of our forefathers; to ask us to reflect on the wrongs we do to each other in community and see how they may be put right. For the putting right of a wrong is the golden thread that unites all these stories and shows how women's influence may sometimes triumph over the worldly power of men.

The Way Beauty Comes Apart is a novel formed of interlinked short stories, whose narrative is composed of the stories of different families and individuals. The reader's view of the people of Nefin is focused, again and again, on the travails of a particular family in a particular location at a particular moment in time. It is a work of immense charm, of revelation and of deep empathy with the people of the past.

*For: Tiff, my daughter
I know we are still in communication—
our stories are for always*

Contents

Deepest thanks and gratitude to those in Wales. To Alis Hawkins for her expertise and exquisite guidance, her bright literary light. To Brychan Jones for his clear-eyed and clear-eared reading, voicing, and wise counsel. To Titus Sharp for his encouragement and commitment to art of place and of nature. And in the US, to Mary Donadoni, the best second pair of eyes out there. To Rachael Stewart, who read these chapters when they were just badly behaved seedlings. To Adam Robinson, Dan Klefstad, Rob Dunbar, and Karen Formanski, who were beyond instrumental in moving this from a completed manuscript to a physical book. And lastly, to Michelle Reale at Ovunque Siamo Press for, among other things, her unflagging belief in the art of writers, the beauty of writing, and the divine meditation of reading

Mae alaw pan ddistawo
Yn mynnu canu'n y co'.

    —Dic Jones

A melody when silenced
Insists on singing in our memory.

    —Brychan Jones and
      Rhian Jones Translation

The Way Beauty Comes Apart

Cranstal Jones • 1876-1904

There was a time—back when I could see the little graves well from behind my bedroom window—that often I stood still as a stork between the curtains and the panes, just looking out. Gwilym said it was too often, but I couldn't stop myself. Three little *beddau carneddau*[*] there were each built of smooth stones, stones which Gwilym had carried up from the strand himself in a jute sack. You can't get a cart down the rocky strand at all, littered as it is with boulders. Each time, I'd watched him empty the sack and pile the small stones, set right the last one, stand back and brush the dirt from his hands. Bow his head. That was him done.

But *I* was not done. I was never done. And in the mornings that followed, I felt compelled to look out to those graves from the moment I woke, even while still abed with the morning light just coming in. Gwilym was already up and out for the day, so I lay in our huge brass bedstead, peering out the bit of window I could see

---

[*]   Grave cairns

and recalling my birthing our babies here. There had been such hope in the pain then.

The word 'bedstead' is a strong, heavy word. And if any bed ever deserved to be called a bedstead, it was our big brass one. How it stood, mighty with its finials gleaming big and round, those finials and the rails too, polished with wax every week so they shone. Gwilym likes to tell how he bartered long and hard with a German bedmaker in far off Cologne to get us the bedstead. How the Germans had the bed all set up for him and then took it apart again, lifted off the finials and knocked out the rails. How they packed it into a crate. The way they told him all the while the value of the brass bedstead, not just beautiful but unscalable and unchewable by any class of vermin and insect. The Germans, he said, wore canvas aprons and assured him in a very proud way that not a single solitary bedbug nor woodworm nor tick would ever scale the bedstead. Nor a mouse. Nor a rat. And all such creatures carry disease, so we were glad to have it.

You've got to keep in mind, now, it's a valuable thing, a bed like that. It's not that our neighbours would have tried to take it from us. No, not at all. But it's best to keep luxuries to yourself when not everyone has the same. Gwilym, being the local shop-keeper, and a successful one at that, took great care not to show off to our neighbours. And so, we kept the cottage simple and plain on the outside. But inside, our place was splendid: lime-washed in ochre every spring to keep it lovely as a painting. The curtains I pulled open each morning were blue *toile de Jouy*, patterned with finger-tall little men and women and children all dressed in farm-ers' clothing. They were busy, ploughing fields or fishing brooks or napping beneath trees with oxen and dogs and milk cows. Whenever I shifted my gaze away from the little graves and turned my face to the curtains, I thought how good it would be to walk into the weave and leave everything behind: the bedstead, the cold blue and white Delft plates, the fireplace crackling and crouching low in the bedroom wall, the dark carved wardrobes that held our clothes, the rosewood music box still wound up and playing Swan Lake. But even if such daydreams were possible, I'd never ever have left behind our three infant daughters who lay beyond the window, just in the shade of the great Wych elm.

Gwilym and I had four children all together. There were our three girls out there, and there was Siôn, our only boy. He was our first child, born too early and alarmingly crooked, bent as an old man. Marged Dafydd, the old midwife, had closed her eyes and said she'd seen it before, once or twice, and that the poor thing wasn't likely to live past the night. But she was wrong. Gwilym thought he'd straighten out over time and was just bent from being cramped in the womb. Gwilym was also wrong. Siôn lived, and lived just as he was, lopsided and cross-eyed, his little chest sunken in like a bog. And that's the thing that made no sense. For while poor Siôn lived, his perfectly formed, fat little sisters did not.

The first time, we couldn't have ever seen it coming. Gwilym and I were delighted and relieved to have a healthy baby after our troubles with Siôn. She was straight and pink and perfect. Her lungs were made for braying and she came out shouting already. The midwife said she'd not seen an easier birth nor a healthier babe than our Elen. She did squall and squall until my milk came in, but that soon righted itself. I was finally getting some sleep now that she was sated, and Gwilym was mixing me a special cordial to help, on the instructions of the midwife, who came with her granddaughter, a midwife in training. The two were wise and helpful. But when Elen was just a few weeks old, Gwilym got up for a drink of water in the night and found her cold in her cradle. I was frantic. But all the panic in the world won't breathe life back into a dead child. Nor rubbing. Nor puffing breath in its little mouth. Both Gwilym and I tried until dawn when the nightjars in the trees ceased their calling and the early grey of morning drove home our waking nightmare.

Cot death is what they called it, those neighbourly women who came to the door with seed cakes and condolences, who arrived with baskets full from here in Nefin* and the farms surrounding. How they whispered, after Elen, as if speaking loudly would draw death's attention to themselves and their own children. As if it might bring the little people to leave changelings for them. When I saw these same women out in the world, they scurried away from me like crabs on the shore. No matter if I were off to the shop or down to chapel. Surely, their hurry was much to do with my dead baby, with cot death. But it wasn't that alone, and I knew it. The other thing that kept them an arm's length from me was this: I'd come from outside. The Manxwoman is what they called me. Gwilym said they aren't so clannish as that and it was mainly in my head. He said that I'm no foreigner if I'm his wife. But Gwilym has always been liberal with the benefit of the doubt.

In the early days, just after Elen died, when I was still quite young and our Siôn was maybe five or so, I committed myself to looking at the bright side of life. I made myself see how flowers still bloomed, birds still sang, food still tasted good. I assured Gwilym that one case of cot death per family would be the limit. That once we'd got through that we'd be clear and done with grief for a good while. Likely done with cot death forever. I said it to myself, as

---

* Nefin is a fictional village in this book, geographically near the very real towns of Nefyn and Pwllheli. The name is also the discarded anglicised, archaic version of Nefyn, which has also been historically referred to as Nevin—and so, in this context it represents a shadow-place and a play on words, a nod to both permanence and impermanence

well. "Cranstal," I said, aloud and like a lunatic, "many a woman has lost a child and gone on to lead a snug and content life—and so will you. Think now of old Gran Quale back on the Isle of Man, think of her and how her boy-child went down the well—and yet, there she was smiling at you over the dining table. Think of Bethys Jones here, down the road, who lost the twins to the red rash and went on to have triplets who grew up strong." These little talks with myself did nothing for my grief—not really, for grief walks alongside you not caring what you say about it—but they did help me with things in general.

Then, after our second baby girl, Esyllt, died just the same, I wondered if I'd jinxed myself, thinking like that, but then I righted myself and reckoned surely two would have to be God's true absolute limit. It was beyond the pale to be sure, and in return I felt as if we should be spared from tragedies, all and sundry, from then on. But I didn't utter the words so as not to bring any ill fortune down on our heads. I put dough in the crevice on the wall to feed the little people—though Gwilym didn't approve—and kept a crock filled with cool water for them too, just in case, so I knew it was never them harming us. If they were real, I treated them too well for them to do us ill. Oh, we knew them well on the Isle of Man—and they are known here as well—though the Welsh call them differently. I'd have suspected them, but it was clear to me my daughters were not switched with changelings. Anyone could see that. They were too healthy looking, even dead. That was my reasoning. Gwilym said he knew it wasn't them just because they simply don't exist. That he was a man of science. No matter what was causing it, I felt we had suffered enough and should be spared from then on.

But then there was the third.

We'd held back naming her and knew her just as Baby. Scared as we were that it might happen again. After she left us, I found that if I closed my eyes, all three of them were impressed behind my eyelids. Each in her own birch cradle, moonlight coming in under the hem of the curtains onto the flags. Like they'd been in their brief stays with us. And in this, my mind's eye, I saw Gwilym and myself—the mother and father—as we'd been, helpless and useless no matter how we fretted.

Now that we'd had such terrible trouble come three times, people in Nefin weren't just scurrying away anymore, they were galloping. But whenever they stood still for a moment, they were looking out at me from under their caps and hats. It was clear I'd become their Job from the Bible, and so there was some pity and some queer sort of admiration in their eyes, but they weren't coming close.

You'll find it's not so interesting, though, when you've got a heartache like this, to read people's thoughts. Nothing is interesting anymore because inside you something has turned to water and floated away, and you don't care anymore what they do. If they were to walk over to you on their hands—like circus performers— feet in the air, spitting chicken feathers, you'd hardly notice it but to yawn and go lie down somewhere quieter. And if they were kind and took you up to rock you in their arms, if they petted your hair like you were a child of God, you'd hardly feel that either. Because you'd know something most do not. That there are no limits to troubles. But the neighbours wouldn't know it yet, they'd have to believe what happened to you wouldn't happen to them.

And there's something more in my case. Some of them— Gethins and Evanses, and Morgans to be sure for I could see it plain in their faces—well, I *knew* they suspected that maybe, just maybe, it was me, Cranstal Jones the Manxwoman, killing her own babies all along. I could see how they might believe it, too. Because, really, how could anyone lose three in a row like that? It was unheard of.

Yes, I was sure they were hissing about it in the cart on the way to market and humming it in the pew. I felt they were turning my possible evil over like a hot oatcake in their hands as they went to bed at night. I saw it all in my mind's eye, a whole story made entirely of my pain, more entertaining than playing cards for them. There was the wife Morgan flopping over to her husband on her best goose pillow, wondering aloud what in the name of God ever possessed Jones the Shop* to think he needed a *foreign* bride when he could have had his pick right here. 'Too good for us is what he thinks he is,' I imagined her whispering to the husband, 'and her from that island known for wickedness and mischief. If you ask me, Jones has made his own bed up there.'

Then I always imaged that same Winifred Morgan getting up to check her little girls, all three safe in their bed. All rosy and breathing. I knew their names and I could almost see them in their nightgowns in the big bed they'd share, the youngest no more than a babe and the eldest maybe four. They might have been my girls' playmates had mine lived. But now they were just reminders.

Oh, how I heard my neighbour women as I lay my own head on the pillow, in my thoughts. That's in my head, sure enough. But I also heard them clear as a bell out in the world while they were gossiping together. They thought I didn't understand Welsh. But wrong, they were. I can get the gist sure enough. They forget I'm hearing Welsh coming out of Gwilym day and night, even though we use English when we want no small misunderstandings betwixt us.

---

*   A nickname that differentiates from others with the same surname

BACK WHEN WE LOST Elen, little dearling of a girl, I told Gwilym I couldn't bear her to be put far from me in the graveyard down the hill in the village, alone and surrounded by strangers. Gwilym said 'Cranstal *fach*,* my very own *mam and dat*** are down in that churchyard, and family can never be strangers no matter whether they've met or not.' I said he was dead wrong and they *were* strangers to a little baby who never met them. I said she needed to be near her mother.

Gwilym was always kind to me then, and so, in the end, he agreed to bury Elen under the branches of the Wych elm, near the collapsed well out in the back garden. It was hard digging to be sure, considering how that tree's roots spread. He had to chop right through some of them. Gwilym had on a blue shirt and a grim look and he sweated over the spade, digging and chopping alone there with the midges at his eyes and nose.

And once we had Elen buried there, it wouldn't have been right to split the dear little girls up. So, regular as a skipping clock— once every two or so years—Gwilym dug again. And it tore reason from the fabric of the world in which I dwelt, like tearing oxen and rivers out of the curtains, like scattering them to the wind.

NOT MANY KNOW THIS, but a cradle can be made into a coffin. All it takes is adding a lid. It's reassuring. Far more reassuring than a standard coffin banged together by Evans the Box in his coffin workshop. I asked Gwilym to leave the graves wide, to keep from packing the earth tight, so that perhaps, somehow, I could let myself think the cradles would rock to soothe the babies. He said

---

* Little—a term of endearment, *fach* or *bach* is used, dependent on gender of noun
** Mom and Dad

it wasn't really possible because earth will pack on its own. But he said he'd try. It might seem the waste of a good cradle, the burying in it, but I couldn't bear to think of putting a new baby into the cradle another had died in in case there were some kind of illness lingering there. If we hadn't buried them in their cradles, I'd have burnt those cradles in the hearth. Couldn't risk the bad luck, even if it was a family cradle. Some would say it's costly, using up a cradle that way, but no more costly than coffins.

Gwilym was agreeable to using the cradles. For while he's a serious man and a champion at barter and travel, he's not a hard man. Sometimes he cried beside me, rubbing his hands on his thighs and his face puffing. His eyes made big fat tears, and they slid down from his chin onto his trousers leaving wet patches. I'd comfort him as much as I could.

It was maybe a year after our last little girl was taken by death, that he decided to get strong on me. One day, just after he'd finished a crying spell, he stood up straight as a poker, looked me in the eye, and said I must close the curtains every night. You see, I'd been leaving them open to be closer to the babies. 'Cranstal fach,' he said to me, firm as you might be with a donkey, 'it's not good for you to keep staring out the window at them all night.'

I patiently explained to him that the fabric over the window was like a veil between me and the girls, driving me mad and I couldn't have it in between. I said he could close his eyes if he didn't like to see the window there. It's easy enough to do.

'Cranstal,' he snapped back at me with his eyes looking tired, 'you must understand that *your* sanity is not the only sanity that matters. Cranstal, do you hear me?'

And, of course, he was right. And of course, I heard him. I heard every single word he said, but it was impossible to answer, because though he had stopped crying for the night, for *that* night, I had never even truly begun to cry. *Never.* People, even people so close to you as your husband, will think you are somewhere alone crying just because you've locked yourself in a room or gone running up the hill and come back looking sad and rumpled. But they assume too much. My tears wouldn't come. They were stuck like milk in a clogged teat.

Gwilym said things to me every night before we went to sleep, things meant to help me, meant to stop me from all the crying he thought I was doing.

'You know life can be hard,' he said, 'but things will right themselves; you'll see.'

'Be strong, Cranstal fach,' he said, 'for me.' I nodded to make him feel free to stop opening his mouth, but inside my skull was splitting in two. And as soon as he fell asleep, I came out of our bed, walked to the big window, and dragged the curtains open wide, holding the lantern light up to the window to see out under the tree. But it was never any help. No light from inside could travel so far as that. Dark night is dark night. Still, I tried, squinting against the lantern's glare on the window glass, struggling to see. We had no gravestones, only crosses made of alder sapling tied with twine, stuck into each pile of stones. I knew how it looked, but unless it was a clear night and a full moon, I could see naught of it. Once I gave in to not being able to see out there, I held the lantern close to the curtains to look at the toile horses there. I was careful not to catch it all on fire. And this strangeness was my way every night. Gwilym never woke when I got back into the bed, not even when I climbed over his legs to get to my side against the wall. Our son Siôn was fast asleep in his little bed down the hall. And I was likely the only creature awake for miles—outside of foxes, owls, nightjars, and such.

It was in that hard time that Gwilym made his yearly long trip to get stock for the shop and whatever else he did when he was away—some mix of trading and banking and bartering. It meant leaving Nefin, travelling along but not over the three rival peaks, across high meadows, down steep roads, past our sister-village Nefyn, and then some distance to Pwllheli. The dock at Pwllheli is nothing like the grand shore at Doolish—for one, there's no long promenade to speak of. And as I'd always done, I stood at the quay waving until he and the ferry were out of sight. Putting on a brave face so he'd not hesitate to go. And then feeling sad to be left behind here in Wales, so small against the mountains and vastness with the curlews calling all around. I'll have you know Wales is monstrous huge to a woman from the Isle of Man.

Here in Wales, you don't see wives go sailing off with their men, nor leaving their holdings much at all but for the market. Most have too much work to do in the home to look up from it except for chapel days. Going to see him off was as close as I got to sailing away. I'm not carping; of course, someone had to stay back with Siôn and the girls.

All the early years of our marriage, because Gwilym was successful in his trading and shop, I thought it might be good to have some help with the housework, bring on a housekeeper. But Gwilym didn't like to have paid help. He said that would make it look like we were *'gwell nag eraill'** and that would have made us no friends. I told him I was short of friends as it was and had nothing to lose so we might as well enjoy the money, spread it around. But he wouldn't have it. And generally, away he sailed not having it.

But this time, when Gwilym sailed away after the last cot death, things would be different. First of all, I felt utterly relieved. I had come to understand that when he was away I could do as I liked, no one to make suggestions or comment or worry. Once I returned home from the quay I flung the curtains open wide, and

---

*   Better than others

I left them that way, day and night while he was gone. Only a thin pane of glass stood between me and my girls while I slept. I heard the rocking of cradles in my dreams. And though my milk had long since stopped, my breasts ached again. And so, I slept without my nightdress, without plaiting my hair, without a cap. It helped me in a way. I was still grieving, but I was doing so in my natural state, which, though no less painful, is better.

Siôn was the child who got lost in it all. My poor only boy. For years, I'd barely seen him—only, it seemed, from the corners of my eyes. A flash like a minnow. A crooked little boy wriggling beside me at the window. A crumpled little figure creeping into my bedroom to overwind the music box.

Sometimes I had fogotten to feed Siôn his supper or to pare his fingernails. That's likely why despite what he said before about everything returning to normal, and about not having help in, Gwilym must have went and outright hired that local girl with the red hair without even speaking to me about it. She appeared on the doorstep two days after he'd sailed off, barefoot with her Sunday shoes wedged under her arm and a bag of her other belongings on her back. She said she was meant to cook and clean and to watch over Siôn. And to keep me company. But mostly to give me a real rest cure. And she was surely right about that. Once she came, I could stay in bed all the time.

She had long square fingers, and she smoothed my coverlet and brought me fresh water in the cut glass jug. She held a ladle to my mouth so I could sit up and sip and then lie back down. Yes, this Yolanda poured the water for me. She pulled the curtains closed, spreading the oxen and farmers and horses out away from each other, increasing the distance. But when I asked her to open them again, she did, for a little while. As a matter of fact, for a while, she did everything I asked her to do. It was like being back in Doolish when I had a bad stomach or a headache and my mother brought me hot water bottles and weak tea. I'd forgotten how nice that was. Yolanda dosed me with valerian to calm me, sitting on the edge of my bed with her knit brows and pursed lips. Worried, she was. She'd taken to wearing aprons like she was a proper cook, not just a nursemaid. They suited her, and I told her so. She grinned with pride.

The valerian loosened my tongue. I told Yolanda things I'd not have told my own mother had she sailed over to help me. I told her all about the babies and about how if we were very still and it was a mild night out a person could hear the cradles rocking away under the big old tree. She gasped. I said, don't be frightened. It's better than no sound at all. Yolanda said we should get up, go for a walk, take in some fresh air, but I was far too tired. She said the sun was shining and it was a fine day for health. I promised maybe one day or the next we would walk over to the village and have some eggs and cakes from the shop. As soon as I was back to myself.

After months away, Gwilym came back again, looking hearty and carrying well wishes from my mother and father as well as my brothers, who he said were so big I'd not recognise them if they walked right up to me. He had a brown envelope in his vest pocket which he put into the top drawer of the cupboard. It was full of paper money from all his sales, he said. He had marbles and a mechanical bank for Siôn—a lion that took up a coin with its mouth. And he had crates of goods for the shop, but I never saw those. He'd had them brought directly to the shop. I'd no interest in the shop, none in the least. It was his. What was supposed to be mine was the home and the children.

When Gwilym had shaken off his travel dust and washed his teeth, he came to our blue bedroom where I was resting in bed. He wound the music box, but I told him to stop. I told him to listen to the cradles rocking. He didn't like to hear me say it, and he took himself away to sleep in another room. He said we weren't to be sleeping together until I was better. He said he wasn't about to be driven out of his head looking at me gawping at the window anymore—not even to see it with the curtains closed. And then he shouted at me that he didn't want to hear any more of my grim stories, or see me feeding the fair folk, not ever. He said if I kept on, he'd have no choice but to send for a doctor, and that it was likely if a doctor, a proper doctor, heard my stories, then it would be off to the sanatorium with me for a while, even though he didn't believe in sanatoriums and knew full well we could handle this our own way—if I would just stop telling the stories. Well, certainly I didn't want to go to any sanatorium, or worse, an asylum which is what he may have really meant, so I closed my mouth to him altogether. I was relieved again, and I spread myself out over the whole bed and tried to enjoy all that cool empty space for a little while. But then I began to wonder.

Gwilym did not return to our bedroom. He moved himself to the far room behind the kitchen, small and warm. I've nearly forgotten what the inside of it looks like now—yellow and white striped paper on the walls, I think. It was hot there because it caught heat from the kitchen stove. He's not one for warm sleeping, but there he stayed. With Yolanda on her cot in the kitchen just outside his new bedroom door.

He looked in on me most mornings, rubbing his whiskers, yawning, smiling. He sometimes brought me a cup of tea on a wooden tray and sat on the edge of my bed just like Yolanda did.

And a bit of cake or scone. The cup was blue and white on a saucer. Dalton. He always mentioned it. I didn't care in the least what it was, though to be fair, once I might have. I wondered why he never brought in a second one for himself—why it was only me that was to drink tea in bed.

Sometimes they came in together, Gwilym and Yolanda, trying to be cheerful in a way that looked like they'd planned it ahead of time. More than once, Gwilym put on a too-big smile and pulled me by the arms up from the bedstead. He said he wanted me to eat and drink at the table like a person should. Maybe even to step outdoors and breathe fresh air. But I didn't feel that he truly did want that, not completely. Yolanda would be there nodding. I didn't believe her either. I made myself deadweight and fell back to the covers. And so, he gave up pulling my arms and sat down to tell me what was happening at the shop, who'd come in, what they said, how they looked. Other things I didn't care about at all. What I did care about was Yolanda standing there as if she had a right to overhear private conversations between me and my husband. I told her to leave. Get out. Get lost. Now. She went. Gwilym looked at me wide-eyed and said 'Cranstal, that was uncalled for.'

I nearly said, 'You can go as well.' But I thought better of it just as my tongue wet my lips to say the words. I was stopped by an image of the asylum in Denbigh floating behind my eyes. I wondered if they had more plans.

I'd started to suspect that I wasn't a woman at all any more. Not to anyone. No, I was more like the Moddey Dhoo, that great black ghost dog. It's not a Welsh dog, mind you—it's a Manx dog. And in my black dog body, I lay about, haunting the place alive.

The valerian, which the midwife brought to Gwilym and he handed to Yolanda for me, did calm me, and perhaps too much. My neck went thin and my skull got heavy. I slept, but nothing stopped me dreaming of my poor babies. Rotting away. You can't help it. Whatever thing you try not to think of comes to your mind. No one *wants* to think about babies rotting away like an old apple core or a gammon bone. When I asked him if he ever thought about how they must be faring down there, Gwilym said I must not allow myself such *selfish thoughts.*

What?

'Just stop thinking about it,' he said, as if I hadn't understood him the first time.

There he was, telling me to stop my mind from being my mind. And there I was, thinking about how, when it rained, the rain that seeped underground made them wet. How it flowed under the floor of my blue and white room as we were on a slope. Oh, how I hated him in that moment.

Sometimes, I felt a hitch, that was when I feared perhaps we hadn't been truly certain they were dead. Everyone knows a story or two about a person who's been buried alive. Oh, of course the girls were dead, I said to myself. Hadn't I checked them a hundred times before Gwilym buried them? Death has a look, but still you check.

THE DAY I TOOK Siôn out to see his sisters was a good day. Gwilym was in town at the shop doing his yearly inventory. It was spring and that time of year will make a person feel better, and so I did feel better, better enough to realise I must make sure Siôn did not forget about his sisters. You see, they'd been gone so long I was afraid he'd lose the memory of them, and how sad that would be. Since I'd been feeling a bit better, Siôn had been coming into view for me, sticking close, rubbing my hand. I got up and put him in his good short trousers and a jumper, a blue felt cap. I wore a dressing gown and a silken kimono. I had such fancy things Gwilym brought back, and I reckoned they may as well be enjoyed. I asked

Yolanda to make us a plate of bread and cheddar cheese and sliced apple from the kitchen. Siôn and I had a little picnic there under the elm with the girls very close by. We sat cross legged on one woollen blanket, and I tucked another around our legs to keep warm, as it was a chill day, though sunny. But as they say, fresh air will make you tired. So, I lay down on my back and stared into the Wych elm branches, just budding out like tiny fists.

Yolanda watched me as if she were my jailer; it was a noxious habit she'd developed. Now, I saw her behind my own bedroom window, still as a lintel between the drapes, and it irked me to no end. And back when she'd handed me the plate of cheese and apples, she'd said how it wasn't really for her to say but I shouldn't take Siôn out there like that. She'd looked me in the eye to make the point, but she was right: it really wasn't her place to tell me what I should or shouldn't do. I was the woman of the house, not her. So, I told her just that, but then I felt I'd been harsh. So, I asked if she'd like to come and have a picnic with us. She made her mouth a straight line and she said she wouldn't.

Out there, Siôn and I nibbled our cheese and apple and shivered a little. I told him the story of the great black Moddey Dhoo who wanted only to curl up on the floor in Peel castle and be left alone. It felt good to share something of my homeland with him, something he'd remember as mine and mine alone.

When I was done, Siôn rocked back and forth on his heels wanting more stories, but I thought we should attend to his sisters, not forget them down below the blanket. I had Siôn put his ear to the ground to listen for the rocking. I did the same. A simple game. At first, we couldn't be sure that we heard anything, so we listened harder. And then Siôn yelled, 'Oh, oh, I hear them!' Now, it's not always possible to understand what Siôn says, but that day he was clear as a bell. I told him he was a good boy and a good brother, tickling him under his chin. My mind was coming back to me, and with it, my mothering. I felt hopeful. So, I went inside and dressed myself properly. I checked to make sure there was dough for the little people in the kitchen. Yolanda had replaced it with fresh—she was more worried about them these days.

When Gwilym came home in the late afternoon, he looked relieved to find me out of bed and dressed. I could see he thought everything was on the mend. But just before supper, Siôn pulled him by the hand to go and listen to the 'rocking sisters' who lived by the well. Siôn was so eager and pleased with himself.

I walked to the cupboard to take a blanket to spread under the tree so we could all sit down there. I fastened my hair up neatly. I put my mouth into a smile.

'Let's go and see the girls,' I was saying as I carried the blanket to the door.

That's when Gwilym went stark raving and did what he never should have. He pounded his fist on the table and kicked a chair over. He ripped the blanket from my hands and threw it to the ground. Then he went out the front door and slammed it shut behind him. I went to follow him, but he was down the hill before I could open the door and see the back of him. I wouldn't allow myself to look mad and chase him into town. The only thing I could do was go to my bed to lie down and wait for his return. And he did come home soon, but not alone. He'd knocked doors and rounded up neighbour men with their long-handled farm shovels and two lanterns between them, though it wasn't quite dark yet. They followed Gwilym under the elm like a little mob of constituents.

I couldn't believe what I saw next. They were digging up my babies in their cradles, like lifting potatoes. I pounded on the bedroom window to make them stop, but they ignored me. Or perhaps they couldn't hear me, as they had rags tied like masks over their faces. But I think it was that Gwilym had told them I was mad. Had told them I was off to the asylum any day now. I pounded, though, and I shouted. I tried to leave my room to stop the desecration, but the door was locked from outside, and I heard Yolanda drag a chair under the handle, saying nothing. Though I could hear her crying as she did it. I screamed that I'd kill her dead. I'd throttle the life out of her!

When I heard her walk away, I quieted and stared out. The men all looked the same in the coming dusk, in their flat caps. I could hardly tell Gwilym from the others as they loaded the cradles into a hay cart. I could barely see the dark pony there with the sun setting, waiting to pull. But I heard the man chuck to the beast. I heard the wheels roll to pull the cart away. I knew straight away that they had to be taking my girls away to the graveyard at the old chapel. The one falling in on itself up above on the hill. It had to be, because the reverend down in town would have nothing to do with this kind of mischief. I knew these men had no thought for doing things properly; they'd pack my girls too tight down into the earth, so they couldn't rock. I screamed through the glass at them. I pulled down the curtains and threw the rod to the floor. It wasn't enough. I picked up the rod and beat dents into the brass bed, beat the wooden furniture into wrecks and splinters. I did not break the glass of the window, though. I knew if I did, they'd lock me away. No question.

In time, Yolanda opened my door and edged her way in to offer me whatever she could—whiskey, valerian, some kind of bitter liquid. I slapped her hands and her face. I pulled a good deal of her red hair right out of her traitor's head. But she was much, much stronger than I, and she *cwtshed** me so I couldn't lash out. Her arms were tight around me, pulling my head under her chin. In the end, I sipped the liquid, let it burn down to my gullet, let

---

* A loving cuddle or hug

it drip down my chin. My legs shook and shivered, and finally, finally I cried. It was a heaving cry that made each breath hard to pull in. And I sputtered like that for the best part of an hour, there in the arms of Yolanda, who smelled of sweat and of spilled black medicine from wrestling me—and of honey somehow. I hated her for watching me break. And then I slept.

In the dark of early morning, I climbed out of bed, crept to Gwilym's hot yellow room, and begged him to bring them back. I asked nicely. I even cried, as I could cry now it seemed, freely. Then I dropped to my knees to plead. But no matter what I did, he said no. He held my face in his hands as if he were arguing with a small child.

He took in a great breath, and then in one long sigh told me what was going to be: 'No, if you want to see them, Cranstal, and I know you do, well then, you need to get yourself better first, and when you get yourself better, then we can go to the old grave-yard together and put flowers on the grave like proper parents do because people don't belong buried behind the house; they belong there in the graveyard.'

'They aren't people, they're *babies*,' I growled at him. He only looked the other way. I knew then that he would not bring them back. Not ever, and even if he'd wanted to, the townspeople would never have looked the other way now that he'd involved them.

There would be no moving him. And if I tried to right things myself with a shovel I'd be put away. My baby girls were gone from me and, in a different way, my husband was gone from me, too. There was no one to speak for me, and when I spoke for myself, no one listened. On top of all that, in the next room, stirring some boiling pot or wiping the sticky face of my son with a damp rag was the red-haired girl who would soon replace me one way or another. I knew it. I had no choice, then, but to come to terms with everything that was wrong. To fix it.

I made up my mind and immediately and completely endeavoured to stay out of bed for hours at a time and then increase it. I weaned myself from valerian until my head was clear of it. I ate my food until my clothes fit me well again. I got up and made my own tea. I gently closed the curtains in the evenings and opened them in the mornings. Like a normal person. I made sure to brush and arrange my hair which is always a sign of wellness in a woman. And I even gave some of my dresses to Yolanda, good ones. I said it was to thank her for everything she'd tried to do for me when I was very ill. She'd have no bad reports of me to carry to Gwilym. Not a one.

I watched her and smiled and wound the music box, let it play Swan Lake over and over. I watched her and did leg raises, leaning against my bedroom wall like I was a ballerina. I was strengthening myself, and it worked. When I got stronger, I took small walks around the garden with its smoothed-over holes there under the elm.

Each day I ventured a little further and felt a little more like my old self, the one Gwilym had liked enough to bring over and marry. The one he liked still. I looked in the mirror and saw I was her again—at least in the face and countenance—all dark hair and smooth skin, nothing rumpled or ruined. But of course, what he saw, what he believed he saw, was ridiculous. A person can never change back, a person can only ever keep changing. I was neither the young and supplicant Cranstal now, nor the confused wreck in the bed. I was something altogether differently made.

Soon, I was having tea and supper at the dining table, talking about the weather, and asking Gwilym about the newest Delft pattern, would we have it in stock soon? Was it *as* blue as years before? He looked so relieved. Soon, he was back in the bed in our room with me, snoring away like he had since the day we were wed. It felt good at first because he was not in the yellow room next to

Yolanda, though that didn't mean so much as I'd thought it might. In my bed, he took up too much room and set my teeth on edge when he reached for me. I chewed the insides of my mouth.

During the days, I brewed cup after cup of tea and served *bara brith** and butter to Siôn. I helped him to adjust his leg braces. I stroked his hair.

One day when Gwilym was at the shop, I put on my overcoat and shawl as it was cool Autumn, and I walked to the old grave-yard. It was not too far, and I knew the way, though soon I felt a bit winded and realised I'd probably overestimated my strength. I kept going up slope, just slowly now.

Their graves were not marked. But I knew it was them, my dear girls. Three, all little and all in a row. New. There were old graves all around. No one else was there, so I sat with the babies for a long while, and I told them the story of the Moddey Dhoo again. I told them the difference between Manx and Welsh little people and how to keep each content. I told them stories of the lives they might have led. I crawled on my hands and knees without shame, picking speedwell and forget-me-not and violet that grew in between the old graves until I'd gathered enough to twine three tussie-mussies,** which I put, one over each of mine. I sang them the lullaby in Manx. To help them sleep.

> Oh, hush thee my dove, oh hush thee my rowan,
> Oh, hush thee my lapwing, my little brown bird.
> Oh, fold thy wings and seek thy nest now,
> Oh, shine the berry on the bright tree,
> The bird is home from the mountain and valley.
> *Oh, horo hi ri ri. Cadul gu lo.*

---

*   Welsh fruit loaf
**   A small bouquet of flowers and herbs tied with a ribbon or string. Victorian

All around me were old graves in this old graveyard. Old. Old. Old. Graves of centuries and centuries gone by. Graves of Nefin long past. Priddys with one stone marking many, poor as they were. Morgans with big stones and deep lettering. Williamses and Gethins, Joneses and Evanses, Davies and Couches. Old Joneses, too. Joneses I'd never heard of. There are none of us who won't become dust. None of us who escape grief. I knew that, but some get more than their share. I'd had more than my share. So, had my girls. It can't be right.

Too soon, it was time to walk back home. But my legs were so very tired. I knew by how the swifts began their evening flight that it would be dark within the hour. I heard the nightjars begin their calls, and a red vixen passed by me, yipping to her cubs somewhere in the gorse. But I couldn't go home to the empty window and the small talk with Gwilym about prices of fabric and the weather coming across the sea, his eyes flat with waiting and yet ripe with hope. His brown envelopes of money and his glee for collecting. I couldn't go back to the hanging threat of the asylum. To Yolanda strutting about in my cast-off dresses with her bosom heaving. To chapel full to the gills with healthy children, the Morgans and their three beautiful, delicate daughters named for flowers, the Priddys and their hardy brood, and the Dafydd midwives, circles under their eyes from delivering babies day and night up and down the countryside. To all the babies who would live to be adults, live to be old men and women. Live, live, live. To look upon all that goodness while everything my daughters would have become lay buried here with night soon to fall over it all yet again. And again. And again, endlessly until the end of time. No, I could not walk home, not back to that. And still, I could not remain in the grave-yard, myself. Deserted as it was, there was still a chance someone would come across me and think me mad, report to Gwilym.

I won't say more that might upset you. Except just this—to say that the graveyard was too close to the sea cliff for safety or reason. And to say that something like gravity pulled me over to it.

The Nature of Godly Visitors

Carwen Priddy • 1873-1908

It's a funny thing, it is, when you find that you have been right all along. And when finally, after all that being right, everyone else—who was wrong for so long—changes their minds and becomes right, too. If you are a certain sort of person, this change in them can make you resentful and contrary. Why should those late comers get the same reward as you, you'd ask. Rankles the pride, it does, to watch them finally catch up and then act like they thought the same as you all along. It could make a person lash out, behave badly, a thing like that. But when *God* is the topic, then you just can't be small about it, can you? No. You must be joyful and welcoming no matter how peevish you might feel. That said, pretending is one good way to get started. Until you can dig deep into your soul and find that welcoming joy, no matter the state of the wretch who has come to the door, swing that door wide open! Praise Jesus—this very thing is what I did during the revival and from then on. I swung that door wide for all, praising God, though I'd been on the Big Man's side all my life unlike those others. They know who they are. But since you don't, I'll say: it was the Evanses and Joneses, but above all the *Morgans*, him with his big job at the quarry. Their manner makes me wonder if they come to *capel** just to be seen, particularly their eldest daughter who, though a child, parades in her fine clothes. I do hope I'm teaching my own to have more sense and goodness in them. But pride goeth before a fall, and while that's a quote fitting for the Morgans, I've also got to remember it myself. I do try.

Oh, and you should have seen me, though, I truly was as manifest in God as was our very best evangelist Evan Roberts himself, though he did never make it this far north, which is a shame.

Good Joseph Jenkins did make it to Nefin, though, and he carried the revival along like a smouldering volcano in his truest of hearts. A minister of the highest order. Though some say he didn't hold a candle to Evans, I say how would they know? They've never heard Evans. Now, I heard Minister Jenkins speak in our little village, on the steps of the capel. He'd been from town to town and village to village like a bee to flowers, spreading the good news, but he spent more than one day at our capel, and I believe it was a particular favourite of his, though he would never say if he had a favourite at all. It wouldn't be seemly. We are all, every last one, equal in the eyes of God! But Joseph Jenkins is a man and so he would have a favourite, and I do still think we were his favourite.

He was a neat man, then, with trimmed fingernails and a tidy silhouette, double buttons on his jacket and fitted trousers that looked to be made of gaberdine. His voice was like that of an angel, I thought, smooth as honeyed wine might be—but we wouldn't know as there are no wine drinkers here among us. God does not move us to drunkenness and Joseph Jenkins does as God

---

*   Chapel, some characters use 'capel' and some use 'chapel'

directs. Wine and spirits are only the Bad Man's temptation away from the true bliss of Jesus. Know that.

Minister Jenkins stood right on the steps, for that day on which he came there were too many to fit inside the capel—and he told us of how God had an regular habit of waking him at midnight and keeping him up until five in the morning.

People gasped, the entire crowd did, all at once, surprised as they were at the idea that God should be travelling about so late at night and early in the morning like that. The more slothful were likely wondering if they themselves had slept through God come calling at their house. But they were wrong; they didn't miss a thing—God won't come calling to just anyone, and if He does come calling to you in the wee hours, He will be certain to wake you. I don't see Him tiptoeing around, shy. No, those gaspers didn't sleep through God's visit; they just weren't yet worth His visiting. There are a lot of people in Wales these days, and He's not coming to just anyone.

As Jenkins told his story of God's visit with one foot on the top step and the other two steps down, looking as if about to ascend directly to heaven, I was enjoying myself and feeling full of the Lord's light. But then I noticed Twm Gethin, leaned right up against the side of the capel, jerking himself awake every once in a while, but mainly just sleeping through Minister Jenkins's telling of just how he poured his tea when God came calling. It was with a shaking hand. How God took tea with Minister Jenkins is important and you could see Twm Gethin doesn't give a fig, it seems, and sadly he will get what's coming to him. Unless he repents, of course, for in Him all can be forgiven, even Twm Gethin who sleeps through God's glory on purpose and without an iota of shame. According to Minister Jenkins, I should be calling Twm Gethin 'Brother Gethin,' but I've a hard time bringing myself to do it.

It's easy to see that God came to Minister Jenkins because of how Minister Jenkins is, how he is neat and pure and how he has bright eyes that seek out and correct evil. Minister Jenkins never has dust on the cuffs of his trousers, nor are his whiskers messy, no, in fact, he shaves them clean more than once each day, I believe, so that he is just-so in the presence of God, whenever God should want to visit unannounced.

Now, God had come to me as well, even before he came to Minister Jenkins actually—truth be told. It was also in the wee hours of the morning, and I heard Him as clearly as I hear you now. More clearly, actually. God has a right pleasing voice, but it is not soft. It's more like the sound of a great bear, and smoky, like the burning of the bush is still upon it. Which makes sense, because in the time of God, the burning bush might not be so very long ago. And once Wales had its share of bears, so my husband says. It only makes sense that God would have a certain raspiness in the throat. God doesn't ask many questions; He mostly just says what He has to. Not much new, mainly things already there in the Bible, but I suppose He has to keep reminding us to remind each other. I do think He picks us pure ones like Minister Jenkins and me to visit so that we can remind the rest. When He talks to you, you feel kind of floaty—I mean I do, and I suppose that's how it is for anyone. I feel floaty and free from time in a way. I can never remember the exact things He has said, but I remember the gist of it. God must want it that way. The floaty gist.

I told my Huw about God coming to me after the first night it happened, and Huw told me it was most certainly a dream. A dream, my foot! I know a dream when I have one, I said to him. I told him again after the second night God came visiting and he told me again it was a dream. On the third night Huw still insisted it was dreams I was having, but he did ask me if God said anything about him, the nosy parker. I said, no, just the usual, His worries about the world as it is and His promises for those who keep His ways and would I please tell people that Jesus loves them. It's not so much what God *says* when He comes visiting but that He's there at all. It's like the warmest visit you've ever had.

After the third night, I told Huw that God had surely noticed that Huw had not been in capel regularly and that, as he had such a wife as me, to whom God made visits, he might well consider mending his ways. Then Huw told me I should keep it to myself, or else folks would think I'd gone mad, and that included him. Mad like Cranstal Jones but she had a reason and I didn't. I didn't appreciate that comparison. Rest her soul, but Cranstal Jones was an odd one and I'm not altogether sure she didn't have a hand in her own troubles.

Mad? Well, God had told me to spread the word, so I just said, 'So sorry, Huw bach, but when it comes to me listening to you or to God, it won't be you I'm choosing to obey—it'll be Him, every time.'

He stood without moving, with his arms crossed over his chest and his eyes in a squint.

'I shall do his bidding!' I shouted, raising my hands to the heavens, and it felt good. Huw turned and went out the door. I didn't chase after him because I knew he'd come to his senses sooner or later. I just took out my bowl and measure and got to baking seed cakes, for I liked to have seed cakes and honey on hand—a treat for when God came as there's no special occasion that'll top that. I think I was well within reason to have a seed cake if I liked it when sitting with God. God never wanted any, and I don't think God does eat—or drink tea either—but I always offered so as not to suppose what might not be supposable.

I did keep on at Huw, though. Some call it nagging, but really it's just caring. Caring a lot. Finally, praise be, he got in the cart with me and started coming to capel regular. I was overjoyed and relieved beyond measure, for I didn't want my husband going to hell all alone. Can you imagine? Me up there and him down below? If a woman is going to save anyone, she's got to—at the least—start with her own husband.

I kept my Bible under my pillow in those days so that God, when He came upon me suddenly, could see how much His Word meant to me. Also, keeping it so is sort of like an extra prayer in your sleep. Now, if Huw tried to make some kind of romance with me, or such, I'd warn him that the Bible was there, and God might not like it so much, what he was attempting to do was right on top of the Holy Book. He said if God could see everything, he'd have seen plenty of goings on and wouldn't be much shocked by anything happening in our bed. He also said didn't the Bible say be fruitful and multiply.

'Not while he's in the room, you don't!' I said.

'But he's always in the room, it seems.'

Sometimes Huw kept at me and just wouldn't give up. In that case, I'd make him wait while I removed the Bible and slid it under the bed out of respect. I always did it with a sigh, though, as we already had five children.

Some nights Huw stayed up with me, waiting for God. Now, I wasn't supposed to know he was up. He pretended to sleep on his side, but I could tell by his breathing and his not-snoring that he was awake. You'd know because Huw broke his nose six times in his boyhood, and that means he can't take a single sleeping breath without letting out some kind of snort or snore. So there lay Huw, quiet as a mouse. I suppose he wanted either to prove me wrong or to talk to God himself, whichever came. Could be he was a bit jealous, too—jealous that God was coming to me and not to him as he was man of the house and some men can think like that. But God can't be tricked by the likes of Huw Priddy or anyone else pretending to be asleep. The other thing is, Huw works hard during the daytime, so most nights, despite his desperation to wait up, he fell to steady snoring before the moon was high at all.

Huw said he felt funny with God coming to our bed—ill at ease—and would I arrange to meet God somewhere else, instead. Maybe in the front parlour? Or better yet, down by the stream. Or best of all, over at my sister's house. Then Huw laughed like he'd just told the best joke of his life. I told him it was no laughing matter, that he'd not be laughing so loudly with the flames of hell licking up his heels!

He was a good man, but on the whole, I was unequally yoked to Huw Priddy and being yoked so meant I did all the pulling where God was concerned and he just sauntered behind looking at the sky and the meadow flowers and at rocks and stones. It worried me because no man can get into the kingdom of heaven on the coattails of his wife. And as if to make me worry more, when Joseph Jenkins finally came to town again, that hot July, my Huw was nowhere to be found. But I couldn't be late hunting him down. There was no time to waste on looking for him behind trees and fishing along the stream. No, I hitched up our old knobby mule to the cart myself and I drove. I had my Bible in my best handbag, a willow switch in my fist, my children clinging to the floorboards as we flew. When I reached the revival, I hardly had mule to post before I was hurrying to get in close to the front, my young ones scurrying behind me.

A crowd of neighbours and people from the next four towns and all the farms between in each direction spilled over and down the steps, but they made room for us, and we crowded in. And what a sight did I see there! Big, strong men, grown pale as ladies with their love for Jesus, pale and weeping. Rows of young maids clasping their hands and wailing fiercely. Old men, bent and curved, suddenly standing tall and leaping for joy! Babis* speaking in tongues.

Someone threw a cat in the air and it landed on its feet purring with joy, and it was passed around to be petted.

'One of God's creatures praises the Lord!'

Minister Jenkins spoke in his best voice, but the people would have gone on as they were without him, for surely, he was only a vessel and they were all in love with Jesus, not Jenkins, though Minister Jenkins did cut a figure. It was a spiritual harvest, I'll say. And I wailed and leapt up with the best of them. I showed Jesus my love, and my children did the same. We pressed as much into the capel as we could and got as far as the doorway. Sun shone in the small window at the end of the capel, and in the spring warmth we all were saved. The famous singing sisters were there, they were, I'd almost forgotten to say. We all sang together, singing 'Tell Mother I will be There' and 'Ride in Triumph, Blessed Jesus.' No rehearsal necessary, we sang and sang and sang. I never felt better in my life. And the glow of that day lasted under my skin for a long time. When Jenkins left us, the people felt as if their heavenly larder had been filled. They knew what they needed to do. Even the Morgans looked convinced.

During that month, men rushed to pay off their debts. My brother, Lewis, returned the hammer and awl he'd stolen from my other brother Llŷr. And he apologised. All the gamblers quit their infernal gambling and so Cal, the *benthyciwr*,** with no one laying odds on horses or dogs or roosters, went broke. And then he left town to where no one knew. The capel rejoiced and declared our town to be a godly town, safe from the gambling sin. And then pubs started going out of business all across the north, for men

---

*　plural form of babi. Baby
**　An odds maker

had stopped drinking. It seemed everyone was changing for Jesus. Everyone. Well, just about nearly everyone.

For some reason though, after the revival with Minister Jenkins, God stopped coming to me. Sudden and leaving no explanation. Instead, he sent me another child. This one I named Emmanuel, which Huw said was a foolish and strange name—not Welsh at all—not even a *smidgen* Welsh. But he didn't go on too long about it, not after I told him it was on orders of God and Emmanuel it would be. It wasn't exactly that God had said to, but more that I knew he would have. See, I did know God well enough by now.

Our little Emmanuel had dark hair and dark eyes, as if he'd come all the way from Bethlehem, himself. And he was a sweet babi, and quiet, unlike my others. Emmanuel smiled early and crawled late, so late that he was carried around on the hip far too long. Huw worried that the babi might be touched. I told him God wouldn't have allowed that unless he had a very good reason for it. And if God had sent us a simple babi, that was because he knew we'd have the strength for it. Huw said the asylum is full of people been sent things they didn't have the strength for. I said they just weren't praying hard enough or looking at it quite right. We didn't talk for a few days that time. And ever since Jenkins last visit, Huw hadn't been back to capel at all. And he'd quit the choir.

And worse than that, the older children were begging to stay back home with Huw, him setting a bad example like he did. Would have been an embarrassment to me that all of the other children from the countryside and the towns were wild to go to church these days and mine not there. Mine turning heathen. But it wouldn't be while they lived in my house.

I had the big boys hitch the mule and I drove us in the cart with determination. I put a big smile on and handed out the seed cakes I made the night before. Seed cakes will cheer up any crowd.

Now Emmanuel, he still didn't speak much, even by the time he was four. But he sang all of the songs, just like a real angel right there in the pew with dark curls down about his little red ears, seated on my lap. And my others lined up in their church outfits I'd made them. Like stair steps, they were.

It was a normal seed cake and capel day with Emmanuel singing and the rest of us as well, when right in the middle of 'Who is a Pardoning God Like Thee?' I felt an itch on my chest. At first, I thought it must have been a crumb of seed cake had gone down my collar and gotten in there, but as I scratched, I felt a lump under the skin. Hard and sharp as a stone. My blood ran cold, for I knew my own mother had had such a lump though I'd never seen it, for she was too modest to show it, even to me, her own daughter. Her lump had killed her.

I prayed right then and there to the Big Man to take away my lump. I prayed to Jesus. I prayed to God. I knew they were the same, but on the off-chance one part was listening more closely than the other, I asked both, and the Holy Spirit, too. If it had been the old days, I'd have prayed to St. Dafydd as well, but in these times that was not done.

I drove the mule cart home from capel as if under a spell, the lump worrying my mind, and me snapping at the children's every question. I even slapped the reins at the poor mule like a heathen might.

That night I took my Bible out from under my pillow and opened it to Matthew. I spread it over my chest to sleep. I thought Matthew would be the book to cure me, if any book could. Huw asked no questions and I said nothing of it. He must have just thought I was onto something more with God.

I felt for the lump in the morning, hoping to find it vanished by the Bible, but it was still there. I pushed at it over and over again. One moment I thought it had grown bigger, the next it felt smaller. And the more I touched it, the redder my flesh became. I told myself to leave it alone for at least two days and not check at all until then. Could be it would go away on its own; stranger things had happened in this world. Could be me touching it was making it worse. It was a struggle to keep my hands away, but I did it.

I put the Bible on it each night. At the end of the two days, finally, I touched it again. It felt the same. I waited another week and a week more of sleeping flat on my back with the Bible on top of me. I prayed every moment in my head.

The day I was sure it had got bigger, Huw reached over across the dinner table and he looked at me questioningly, 'is there another babi coming?' He grinned. I slammed down my cup and ran from the room, out the door. He laughed louder, with his mouth wide open, thinking he must be right. I sat myself down in the dirt outside the front door. I wept. I wept long and hard, grinding my fingers into the dirt, yanking out the little white meadow flowers and nettles that crept too close to the door, yanking them out by their necks. Emmanuel stood in the doorway watching me, quietly. The other children peered out the window, pushing the curtains aside to see me better. I don't know why, but I just didn't want to tell Huw about it. I didn't want to bring it that far.

Finally, Huw came to fetch me with a basin of water. He pulled me to bed and wiped my face with a cool flannel. And despite my not wanting to say, he pried the secret out from me like lifting a stone from the earth, for he was a man who pried stones from the farmer's fields each day of his life. He was a man who worked the earth like no other among us. His brow knitted with concern and with the shock of the difference between what he'd thought and what was. Then he washed my hands and my body as tenderly as a mother would wash her child. He brushed my hair and fed me a seed cake from my handbag with his fingers. He rocked me to sleep. And the next day, Huw drove me to see Doctor Brown in his office between Nefin and Nefyn—up near the Monroe's place. And that was against my will as I wanted to try pure prayer a bit longer. And even more against my will, Doctor Brown had me drink whiskey further fortified with a medicine, enough to knock me flat, and then with his scalpel and razor, he sliced the lump right out and sewed me back together.

'You never know with lumps when you take them out—either they come back or they don't. It was worth the try, now just wait and see. And try not to worry, Mrs. Priddy.'

I was drunk as a lord and hardly able to sit in a chair after it all, but still he grated on me with that 'wait and see'. Wait and see, as if there was no great intelligence at work? No, he was wrong, with all his doctor's education. All his maybe this and maybe that. Truth was simple enough. Everything is up to the Big Man and no one else, and he should have known it and said it. And I would have liked to remind him of it if I could have. Huw carried me out to the cart and made me lay on blankets in the back while he drove me home. When I became sober, the pain was ungodly.

From the day of that surgery on, Huw was worried. He began to wait up at night himself. He said he wasn't sure there was a visiting God, but if there were, he was going to be awake and ready to speak with Him or Jesus. And if neither of them came by but the *diafol** did, he said he'd speak with him too and get this straightened out. I told him that was *not funny* and that the diafol's name should never be said in our home, no matter what. He looked at me queer and said he wasn't trying to be funny. Said he was deadly serious. And his eyes said so too, so I let it drop. Huw prayed aloud at the side of our bed, which was a thing I'd never seen before from him. In the past he'd been a mouther of prayers at best, moving

---

*   Devil

his lips to the voices of others. But now he prayed in a big voice, without shame or embarrassment. He even made the children pray with him. As a matter of fact, he prayed more heartily than ever my own father had when my mother found her lump, and my father, *he* had been a preacher. A preacher but a cold face and a cold hand on him. But that's enough and I won't say more—it's no good to speak ill of the dead. Though I suppose I am one of them now. Forget I said that and remember that we also must take to heart the commandments, and to honour mother and father is required.

How it swelled my heart to see Huw up every night like that, becoming a godly man. I was so proud of him. But in the end, Huw's nights up and his ten thousand prayers did my health no good. More lumps came. Some the size of currants, some the size of grapes, and all of them fixed in place as they were inside my breasts.

And then, soon after, the pain in my stomach began and a great swelling came. And such tiredness came upon me, tiredness like I'd never known before. My eyelids were heavy as slag heaps, but no matter, the pain wouldn't let me sleep. Doctor Brown came to look in on me and said there was nothing else he could do for me, but that I should have whiskey for the pain. As much as I liked. And some of a liquid he handed Huw inside a brown bottle. 'Morphine,' he said. 'But use it sparingly because it's hard to come by and too much will kill.' But he was a fool. It didn't help. It only made it hard to move or cry out.

I suppose I knew it was getting close to the time that I was going to leave this earth and finally get to join with God in heaven, to see Jesus in person for the long run. Not like when He used to come and visit me, but absolutely face to face in eternity. I reckon I should have looked forward to it with pure joy, but no matter how much I believed in Him, I didn't want to go away from my children and my husband. I resented it. Huw said, 'Don't go, Carwen fach. Stay here with us.'

'I'm trying, Huw, I am,' I mumbled.

He raised his hands to the ceiling and said God was a selfish *cachwr** to take me now after all I'd done for Him. I tried to defend God because I didn't want Huw paying for what he'd said, but I was too tired and Huw wasn't altogether wrong. My children tiptoed in and out on Sunday, and I could tell by their faces that they half expected to see me rise and hitch the mule as I'd always done. Half expected to see me pressing seed cakes into the pan. Wanted me to lead them in their prayers as long as I was still breathing.

Huw washed between my toes and the rest of me every night with a warm flannel. Mornings, he washed my face, trying to wipe the dark circles from around my eyes with a cool one. He kissed me more than is normal for him. And he was never cross with me, only with the Big Man.

'Not to repeat myself, Car, but if that *cachwr* takes you now then I'm finished with him and his whole lot, and if I were Catholic, I'd be done with each and every bloody saint as well!'

With a strange rush of energy in me, I whispered to him no, no, that wasn't right. It would be better if Huw mended his ways so that he could see me in heaven when he got there himself. And he wasn't thinking of going Catholic, was he? Because that might present a problem.

He put his fingers through his hair and said, 'Who'd want to live in heaven as it's run by such a one who's responsible for letting every class of disease and destruction run rampant over the poor people of earth day and night, year in and year out? Why's he got to put us through all this?

---

*   A dastardly shithead

'What's the choice?' I whispered. 'You won't like it in hell any more than that, so please, Huw, please don't say those things. Take them back.'

You could see he didn't want to say it, but he did. 'Alright,' he said with the corners of his mouth turned down and his head turned to look out the window and toward the mule who stood braying there, 'Alright, I'll take them back.' While he was in the mood for agreeing, I also made him promise to raise the children in the capel so that we could all be in heaven together and that would be nice, wouldn't it? You can never tell if Huw really means to do what he says, or if he's just making you happy by saying yes, so did my best to point to the Bible and he promised again with his hand on it, good enough for a minister or a court of law. And so, I was satisfied as much as I could be with the disease eating away at me like a shoal of toothed fish. It made it hard to think straight. And there's not a speck of good I can say about that pain. I suffered. And then it became hard to breathe, as if I were drowning.

But after all that fear and all that prayer, I am sad to say I'm not rewarded as a loyal servant yet. I'm not in heaven at all. I'm still here. Still here speaking to you. In the old house, near the doorway. A bit stuck in place but not uncomfortable. Here, where Huw moved my bed to, so that I could watch what was left of that summer with the breeze blowing over the gorse and curlews calling overhead. I have to wonder: have I been forgotten?

The Practicality of One Small Boy

Siôn Jones • 1897-1906

When I walked, I always leant over and lopped and hopped. And when I ate, my porridge sometimes flopped right out of my mouth and off the spoon and down the front of my bib that Yo-Yo sewed out of old flannel and tied so tight around my neck like I was a babi. She did. And I'm not. I'm almost nine years old, which means I'm much too old to wear a bib, of course.

I heard *those words* I didn't like when people said them, even Yo-Yo. Yes, I heard Father say invalid son about me to the man at the train station. He also said only son. And only living child, on top of it. Now, if you don't know what invalid means, it's when your legs are bent up like mine and you are unusual like me. Yo-Yo didn't say invalid, she said *crippled* but she meant the same thing. My hands worked just fine, though, and I could wind the clock and the music box in Mother's room with a pinch-finger. I could take apart the clock, too, and put it all back together before Yo-Yo ever knew it. Lickity splickity. My heart went BLUMP if I heard her coming. For you don't want to be caught by Yo-Yo doing what she's told you not to.

Some days, Yo-Yo let me take out all the jars and tins from the bottom shelves of the cupboard while she cooked some old porridge—which I never liked at all—or washed the dinner plates or polished the forks. She let me play with all of the green beanies and stewie tomatoes, and gherkins and pinky rhubarb fool; the jams and jelly—all colours—but apricot is my favourite. Orange Marmalade is always a surprise because I love it sometimes and I hate it sometimes. But Father says we must not waste it if we take it. Not ever because it comes from oranges and oranges come from far away and are dear. Father is always saying what we should and should not do. But I reckon that's what fathers do.

Yo-Yo, she let me stack and shift the jars and move them all about and then sort them back in. She almost never stepped on me down there on the kitchen floor. And I always was very, very careful in my stacking, of course, because we aren't made of money, you know.

Mother and Father did not lop when they walked, and neither did Yo-Yo, of course, just me. Most people don't lop, and I know this. Though I'm sure there's another boy somewhere who does. I just never met him yet. But I did see a three-legs terrier once, in town, which seemed a bit like me, and I wanted that terrier for my own. But I forgot to say so. Well, I didn't forget, really, it was just that Father and Yo-Yo weren't understanding me, like always. I talked louder about it, of course, but it did no good. But then I thought maybe that terrier belonged to a boy already, and I wouldn't want to take away his pet and make him cry. Some boys have terriers, but not me. Now, I did have a frog, which sounds a lot like a dog and which I kept in a big, glass jar, but then I left him in the sun. *Accidentally.*

I did have a mouse, too, also in a jar, but somehow it got scampered out. Father said, 'One should NOT keep rodents in the house; one should keep rodents OUT of the house!' He said it was the *entire point!* But too bad for him, of course, because he didn't like what happened next. Next, I got a fancy rat in a real iron cage that old Mister Idris Port Master gave me for my ninth birthday. It came all the way from London, on a ship, but in a cage, of course, not like the ratty rats that just hitch a ride. That's what Mister Idris Port Master said. He told me those other rats are called *vermin*, but mine is called *a pet.*

Mister Idris Port Master was Father's bestest and only fancy customer at the shop, and so I got to keep the rat to make him happy. I gave a name to the rat, and that was Mister Idris Port Master, out of respect, of course, for the real Mister Idris Port Master that gave him to me. My rat was fancy because his eyes were red and his fur white as the whitest thing ever, like a snow-flake or a white lady flower—which I don't know the real name of yet—but it's that one that grows tall by the well and smells like Mother's perfume. Mister Idris Port Master rat had big teeth, though, and they were not white *at all*; they were yellow as can be, and could he bite! Chomp! But I never told on him, and really now, it didn't hurt no more than an injection, and the doctor gives me plenty of those, of course. I been getting injections since I was a babi. Anyway, if you ever get a pet rat, just so as you know, they like bits of oat to eat and hair ribbons to play with and climb up on, mostly blue ones. And white, they like white ribbons, too, I should say. And apples. You might think they love cheese but they don't much. They prefer apples.

Sometimes Mister Idris Port Master, the rat one, would go out of the house with me, especially on my picnics with Mother, before she fell down into the water, which I was not supposed to know about. But I heard one person talking about it and I won't say who.

Anyway, my pet rat, he liked to stay in my trouser pocket and only put his head out twice or maybe four times a day because he was a smarty that stayed inside so we wouldn't get in trouble. I knew he really didn't like his iron cage, like I don't like my braces. I always gave him some apple peel and some stale bread from the kitchen, and, well, he shitted in my pocket, but that didn't bother me at all. His crap is only little.

Mother never minded him, but Father and Yo-Yo said—all the time—I must keep him only in his cage and wash my hands if I touch him, *every single time*, which is silly because I touch him *all* the time, 'specially when he is in my pocket! And besides if I used up so much soap as that, then they would say, 'Siôn, that's simply too much soap, you'll drive us out of house and home using the soap like that, and there you are making Yo-Yo run for water all the time. You must stop touching that rat!' They would say it in big, loud voices to the roof! That's what they'd do, alright.

One thing Mister Idris Port Master loved was to do climbing exercises, so I built him a new rampy path each day from broken branch bits and old coming-apart ropes I found in the garden under the big trees in the back. I would have liked to have some people over to watch his tricks, like at a circus. I've never really been to a circus, but Mother told me all about them and said she would take me someday, but she didn't. Even though he had lots of talents for climbing and jumping, Mister Idris Port Master could never be a circus rat because I didn't have an audience and everyone knows you need an audience for a circus. I would have liked a brother or sister to be an audience, but I didn't have any that's alive.

We got tired of being in my bedroom without any audience, him and me. So, on a Tuesday, which I know it was from the Allinson flour calendar Yo-Yo keeps on the kitchen wall, which she doesn't even know I know how to figure, I let him help me move the jars on the kitchen floor. That floor is made of stone and hurts to sit on. Even though he didn't mean it, Mister Idris Port Master bit me once more in my finger. On Tuesday, remember? My finger got very red; this also happened on Tuesday.

On Friday then I got very sleepy and very hot and very very sore on that finger. I could feel a thump there in the tip of it like a little heartbeat. Yo-Yo saw me holding my finger and she grabbed my hand to look at it. She said, 'You have a splinter there, I think,' and gave me a *cwtsh* like she always does. It did look like a splinter, which I've had before, and I was glad she didn't know it was a bite from my rat. Then she heated a needle over the fire and let it cool and she put that needle in my finger to get the splinter out. She kept on and on while I lay in my bed not crying even though it really hurt. She tried not to hurt me, I could tell, and my eyes were so tired it wasn't so bad anyway. Yo-Yo cursed at the sliver that wasn't there—she said the D word a lot of times, and even the F, which we are not allowed to say in this home but which I hear people say sometimes anyway. Finally, she said 'I reckon I got it because it's not there' and she kissed my forehead. She put some burning medicine on my finger and wrapped it up in a white cloth and told Father about the splinter. He said, 'Oh, it will work its way out, and if not, we can call the doctor later. When they weren't looking, I got up out of bed which was hard because I was so very tired, but I had to put Mister Idris Port Master in his cage even though he didn't want to go, so that Yo-Yo wouldn't know he was in my pocket the whole time. I put him in and shut the little door, and it looked like he'd been there all along. But he was cross with me for locking him up. He turned his back on me and went to sleep.

On Saturday, I think it was, I felt so tired that my hands wouldn't move and my eyes wouldn't open. I wanted to go to the kitchen and count the days because the seventh day in the line is always Saturday which is why I like Saturdays, and I also like to see the X that Yo-Yo makes on the day that has passed. She always uses a stubby pencil to do it first thing in the morning—new day comes and old day goes she says. But I just couldn't go to the kitchen because I was too sick, and Mister Idris Port Master couldn't go without me, so neither one of us knew what day that last day was for sure.

The Condition of Love and Affection

Cadog Priddy • 1900-1913

Thirteen years and some more, I was, when I caught the dratted fever. I was the strongest of us brothers and sisters, and the eldest. Yet the fever killed me first, and maybe me only—I'll never know. My babi brother Emmanuel was burning up with it, too, but he was maybe over the worst of it by then. He'd been burning for days and days. We were all a mess of sickness with only my dat to care for us, and him coming down with it, too.

It was the Morgan girls who brought the fever to capel. Dat later said anyone with eyes in their head could see those girls were carrying the germ from how they were far too white and pink in the face, right there in the Morgan family pew. Dat said, just like Mr. Morgan to be so self-important like that, bringing a sick family to capel. Said Mr. Morgan probably knew what was up and was trying to get them into heaven just in case it went bad, or worse just trying to look holier than thou. Making sure they didn't miss a day.

Even though Dat didn't like the Morgans, I liked to look at Lili Morgan anyway, so I saw too how their heads bent heavy on their necks. I saw too that they were ill. And I saw Mrs. Morgan palm her girls' pale foreheads and look worried. But she never did take them from the capel as she should have. No, she just left them to sit shivering up against one another through the long sermon. And it was a long one, indeed, with extra time spent on what might be waiting for us if we didn't live right as well as what might be waiting for us if we did. Maybe Mrs. Morgan reckoned that when the fever is striking, it's no time to turn your back on the word of God, especially in the middle of a hell and heaven sermon. Anyone can understand that.

Now, I fancied Lili Morgan in her small white felt hat and matching white collar. She was by far the loveliest girl in capel and beyond. She had perfect posture, though she was just a girl, and a way of turning down the corners of her mouth as if she were a little displeased, all with her eyes far away. Everyone knew she was mad for London and for all the types of fancy things there, for she'd tell anyone who cared to listen. All the biddies about town believed Lili Morgan had got big-headed like her father. Once, I saw a particular biddie twisting her own big fat owl's head to see into the pew behind her so that she might whisper loudly in a friend's ear that the only way our Lili Morgan was getting to London would be as a nanny—or *worse!* Then that same woman covered her mouth with her hand and whispered even more loudly, 'Jesus forgive me!' I'd seen the whole thing because I only ever half closed my eyes in prayer. I liked to look around and see what everyone was doing. I'd a sharp ear for whispers. And I didn't feel too badly about it either because people were doing a great many things, much worse than sitting there with half-closed eyes and listening in—nose picking, for instance.

Being a nanny didn't sound that bad to me. I supposed nannies would eat well and mainly spend their days playing with little children. There's lots of things worse than being a nanny in London, I'd imagine, so exactly what sort of *worse* did the old gossip mean?

I'd have liked to go to London with Lili myself, to see the sights. To keep her safe from all of the worse things I knew of, like Jack the Ripper. He was never caught, you know. And even though he might be a very old man by now, he would still be dangerous. Yes, I'd like to have held Lili Morgan's hand and walked with her to the pier, us sailing right out of Pwllheli. Us smiling and waving to our families who'd have stood on the pier waving back and crying like mad into their best handkerchiefs. Especially Lili's family.

My own dat and brothers wouldn't cry in public. They'd put on excited and proud faces for the occasion. They'd maybe be planning to come visit me and Lili in London someday. And even Lili's family wouldn't be *too* afraid because they'd know that I was a strong and smart young man, and that Lili would be safe with me. I spent most of my capel time thinking about Lili Morgan and about sailing away with her. I knew we should be married first 'cos it's not proper to sail away unmarried, but I was only thirteen. I wondered if she might kiss me on the mouth, there on the deck of the ship, after we sailed off but before it got dark and we'd have to part for the night.

Sometimes, after capel, while we waited for all the grownups to finish cosying up to the minister, Lili had showed me her magazines, which she kept always in her bag. They were fancy magazines just for looking at the latest thing. Fancy ladies in fancy dresses and hats. There were men, too, in worsted suits and shined shoes, shined to glass. When I saw them, I could feel the thin spots in my own trousers letting in air and the scratchiness of my old hand-me-down waistcoat poking me. When I tried to think of other things,

my toes moled around in my socks, finding where holes were start-
ing, like they had minds of their own.

That's when I feared that the truth was Lili Morgan wouldn't
be caught dead in London with me. With Mam gone a couple
years now and Dat less than handy with a needle, I was a sight. To
give credit, Dat did his best to keep our hair cut with a big set of
shears, but he'd done me so uneven that even Emmanuel—who
was touched by the fair folk—pointed and laughed with his little
teeth all showing. I slapped at him. And I was punished, for no
one was ever to slap at Emmanuel. Now, I remembered what it
was like to be eight, and I knew it was harder for Emmanuel than
it ever was for me because he's so puny he looks like five. So I did
feel bad for slapping him. Him hardly even remembering our mam
at all. But still, he shouldn't have laughed at me. No one likes a
laughing at.

Mam. One day she was there throwing us into the mule cart
and taking us to revival, her bag full of seed cakes; and the next
she was under the covers moaning away in the bed. Dat says the
cancers took her like a thief in the night. And he's right about that.
She was beautiful, Mam was. With light brown hair rolled like a
crown on the top of her head and a nose that turned up but not so
far up you could see inside. I thought she must be the most beautiful mother around. More beautiful than the preacher's wife, who
looked like a candlestick without a flame. Or like Lili Morgan's
mother who always looked like something going putrid in the seat
next to hers was poking its way up her nostrils.

But Mam was not soft. She was not delicate. No, she was in
the service of The Big Man, and so were we to be. She kept us
mended and fed and clean because God says that's how it should
be. She brought us to church because that's how God said it should
be. She took God's rules seriously.

All that Jesus in her mind didn't leave her much time for much else, though. She never did joke with us nor tell us stories, 'cept for Bible stories. I reckon maybe she would have when we got older, but by then she was gone. She was rulish and sternish, but I missed her tonnes. When I sat in capel with Dat, it was Mam's big warm hip bumping into me that I missed. It was the space she took up. Dat did his best to keep us up with capel; but he didn't want it, and neither did we. We were all just doing it for Mam's memory and so that if there's a heaven, we could be let in up there with her. Dat said there's a man named Pascal who figured it all out a long time ago. He goes on and on about Pascal when we are out in the fields picking stones for farmers. I miss how Mam just said, 'you're going because I said you're going.'

Thing is, sometimes I wished The Big Man had taken Dat instead of Mam. But then I'd look over at Dat with his pointed whiskers going grey and his eyes tired, and I'd take it back. The last thing he needed was me wishing the life out of him.

Dat was there with me at capel, us both seeing how the Morgan girls slumped up against their mother. He was three places down from me as we kept the younger ones between us, to keep them quiet. He gave us all the eye and picked up a bound Bible. He thumbed through Leviticus, but Dat cannot read. I wondered what he was pretending at. Lots of people cannot hardly read here, so nothing unusual there. I can, though. I can read because I have learned at school. I'm pretty good at it, too. Schoolmaster says I'm not top of the class, but I'm not bottom neither. I asked him how about London, am I bright enough to go there? He said, 'Well, if that's where you've set your sights, Cadog Priddy, you'd better stop yammering in Welsh as soon as you set foot out the school door like I hear you doing every day. Better get your mouth in the mind of English only.' Some schoolmasters are always like that, trying to crush the Welsh right out of us.

But I never hear the Morgans speaking Welsh much, so maybe there's something to it as far as London goes. But my bigger, my more immediate, problem was what to *wear* to London with a girl like Lili on my arm. I thought if I could just borrow a finer waistcoat from my big cousins down the road who had one between then, then I could wear it to capel next week and give Lili Morgan an eyeful of my potential. Maybe she would fall in love with me and we could strike out together right away. Then Lili wouldn't even have to be a nanny. And certainly, wouldn't have to be worse.

See, I'd like to take care of Lili Morgan whether she ever married me or not. I'd like to chat with her over tea in the evenings and walk through the gardens of the Queen. The Queen has a lot of gardens in London, everyone says. Some of them call her a right colonizing bitch and some of them would love to live under the pits of her arms, but either way, they're all in agreement about her gardens. I'd like to buy Lili all of the darling velvet and silk gowns she ever could want. Darling, she says, *darling*. I could listen to Lili Morgan say darling all day long. My plan was to join Scotland Yard as soon as I was old enough. That way, I could provide for Lili and maybe solve the case of Jack the Ripper. I had some ideas on that, and I plotted them out in our pew with Emmanuel dozing off against me.

But I was shaken from my thoughts by the awful sight of Mr. Morgan standing up at the end of sermon with Lili in his arms, limp as a rag. He carried her down the aisle. It was an odd scene— Mr. Morgan with Lili looking small in his arms, and Mrs. Morgan pulling weakly at the youngest sister Rhosyn, pulling her along by the waist bow of her capel dress. And then the middle sister Eirlys, her not looking sick in the least, rushing the group along, holding Lili's trailing hand. And as for me, I jumped up to follow behind the panicked flock of Morgans, wanting more than anything to offer my help. To be noble. But in what way? I wouldn't dare take

Lili from her father's arms. He'd have trod right over me like I was nothing at all.

If I'd stood before him asking what I could do, maybe—just maybe—he'd have said, 'Aren't you the Priddy boy? I've heard you're strong as a red bull from lifting stones with your father. You drive my cart while I tend to the girls inside it.' Then, just maybe, I'd have climbed up onto the bench, care in my eyes evident to all, and flicked the string whip just urgently enough to get us to the Morgan place in the nick of time. But none of that ever happened because I wasn't strong enough to push through the crowded capel—everyone rushing up to help. The Morgans wheeled away while I was still jammed behind the doors.

Us PRIDDYS, WE CAME down with the fever right away, just after evening meal the next day. The headache came on something terrible and then the fever. Doctor Brown left some tonic outside the door, but he wouldn't come in. 'No use!' he bellowed through the door in the whooshy way that made me know his false teeth were slipping. 'Let it run its course, take the tonic, keep under covers.'

Dat whispered through his chattering teeth for his own self, 'Thanks for nothing, again, Doc.'

Dat talks curt like that a lot. He waited until the good doctor rumbled away before crawling over to the door to open it and fetch in a heavy brown bottle and wooden spoon. One bottle for the seven of us. I said some prayers for Lili Morgan. I spared one or two for Rhosyn, too, as I knew Lili would be very sad if the fever took her favourite sister.

Dat, Emmanuel, Sissy, Cled, Dai, Glyn, and me. All of us were sweating and moaning. Dat and I did our best to take care of the rest and we laid down together last, late that night. We took a tiny sip from the brown bottle here and there, trying to leave enough to go around. The fever had me feeling that I could float up. Like a cloud but only as high as the ceiling. So, I took my advantage and floated around. And I saw Lili Morgan in the room. She was floating in her own bed, draped in old blankets, but because Lili is Lili, she was somehow still stylish. I watched her long curls looping down from her sleep bonnet. She whispered with me up in the corner, where we met up against the ceiling. We made the agreement. And we held hands up there, though we knew full well she was also at her own home, way down the road. Then I heard Mam reading aloud from the Bible. Her voice came from down under the floorboards. She read Matthew and then said she was coming up into the room to kiss Emmanuel goodnight.

She hadn't seen us for such a long time. She was surprised that Emmanuel was such a big boy now and wanted to know why Dat had shorn off his black curls. She looked well. I wanted to ask her was she a ghost or a spirit and had she come down from heaven, and if so, why had she been down under the floor like that? But she didn't look in the mood for questions. She wore a kind of gown I'd never seen before, and she carried an orange cat about her shoulders. That cat looked as if he had some scratch in him even though he purred so loud the walls shook. Mam passed under me, as I was still up pressed to the ceiling, and she offered me a seed cake, reaching her hand up high over her head, motioning for me to reach down for it. But I wasn't hungry. And I only knew how to float up, not how to come back down.

I bobbed there at the ceiling, and yet I noticed my own self shaking on the blankets below. Cled and Glyn, who were only a little younger than me, were dripping wet flannels across my chest and face. Glyn was lifting my eyelids, and Cled put his ear to my mouth. 'Dat,' they said, flatly, together, 'Dat, looks like he's dead now.' I watched Dat struggle over to my bed to look. He hunched there for a while, like a great big crab, still sick with it himself. Then he cried out.

'Carwen, I'm sorry! I'm sorry! I'm sorry!'

My mother and the orange cat, though, were nowhere to be seen now. Lili Morgan was gone, too. Back to her own home I reckon. The me below looked cool and pale. But me up on the ceiling, the real me, I stayed there for a very long time. You'd think it would be boring, but it's not so much.

I've learned how to go up and down now. There are days I float up through where the ceiling itself has upped and gone. I'm not bored, for only boring people get bored. I go straight up into the blue sky for moments and eons and then come straight down again. But no matter how many times I do it or how long I stay, I'm still just thirteen.

56

The Importance of Making a Good Impression

Lili Morgan • 1902-1917

I must tell you I was determined, utterly bound and determined to get to London and make my life there. It had been that way from the time I was a little girl just turned eight years old. I'd say I found my passion the day my school teacher—Mrs. Williams— showed the class her three postcards from London. I will never forget them and the way they made me feel—here were laugh- ing women pedalling bicycles down a lane—here were picnickers watching the polar bear in its cage at the world-famous Zoological Garden—here were busy people crammed into the underground. Oh, how I saw in those three scuffed postcards more sights of won- der than can be seen in our village in an entire lifetime. And I meant to be part of *that* world.

At the age of twelve, I determined my future profession. I would need one in London, and that's when I became absolutely passionate-mad for fashion. And more than that, I found that I was *talented*. Really, from the moment I looked down and realised

I was wearing clothing—and I must have been only an infant then—I'd already had preferences and fashion sense. But once I found out about fashion houses and about fashion *magazines*—and once I read those—I was *smitten*. I soon learned what looked good and what didn't, even to a fault. Add to that the fact that I was already top reader in my class, and so it's no surprise I *devoured* every article and studied every illustration. When other girls asked me to play skipping games or to walk home from school with them, gossiping about the Priddy boy this and the Evans boy that and the other Evans boy something else, I declined, preferring to walk alone thinking about fashion and my future. The other girls always said I was conceited, but I didn't care what they said and just smiled and went my own way.

I was a neat and calm girl, but not a drab one—just serious and particular—perhaps *discerning* is the word. A person who understood that first impressions are forever. And when I first read what Myrtle Lemmin wrote—that *fashion is a place for appearing rather than speaking*—and her so very reserved and quiet herself—well, I knew, right then, I was simply meant to be *en vogue*. Indeed, I was certain that I would become a fashion writer in the Big Smoke—just like Myrtle Lemmin herself but younger and more modern—and when I did, I'd be part of the artistic crowd—I'd finally be understood and appreciated for what I had to offer—and then I'd see my own name in print in the very magazines of fashion I adored.

Now, mind you, I was well aware that getting to London would be no task for the fainthearted. And so, for months and months, almost every day after school ended, I sat upon the stool in the books corner of Gwilym Jones's Afar Shoppe, which is a darling shop with a bit of everything Jones finds interesting but not a grocery or a haberdashery. He spells it strangely on purpose. To draw attention.

I sat there with customers stepping around me—and I read and reread *every* fashion article from every fashion magazine Jones had, and I stared at *every* illustration. I took notes on little cards I kept in my cloak pocket with my pencil, and I promised Mr. Jones I would not crease the pages or ruin the magazines in any way. But that was more difficult than I thought it would be.

In time, Mr. Jones decided it would be better that I come by on the first of each month to take away any old fashion magazines that had not been sold and were so out of date they could not be. He made me a gift of them. That way I could read them at home, he said, instead of blocking up the aisles. I was happy enough to take them home with me instead of reading in, and besides, Mr. Jones was often foul with halitosis, and the smell of it was through his whole shop. His housemaid Yolanda was forever handing him mint sweets from her pocket if she came in. I'm very particular about breath and such.

Now, about the magazines, in this town, out of date meant more than a year gone because Mr. Jones was getting them second hand to begin with, and things just got here slowly anyway. My fashion was always running slightly behind. But there was nothing I could do on that account. I was held captive in my backwater hometown by circumstances beyond my control. Sometimes I lay awake at night worrying that, all of a sudden, our neighbours would develop an interest in fashion and buy all of the magazines, leaving none behind for me. But in the light of day, I knew those worries were unreasonable. I was utterly alone in my interest, and Mr. Jones had a thick stack waiting on the counter each month.

I was invariably out of breath when I rushed into the Afar Shoppe to get my copies of *Vogue* and *McCalls* and *La Mode*. When I came hurrying to the counter, Mr. Jones invariably had *his* nose in some magazine—usually catalogues of goods and where to find them or else something called *The New Age*—which he said was entirely about ideas and philosophy—like fashion for the brain, he said. He would put his magazine down, give me his same old smile, and hand me my package all wrapped up in brown paper and tied with a white string. I never opened it until I got home; I *loved* not knowing exactly what was inside until I was alone and no one could bother me.

At home, I kept a wooden crate divided with sheets of thick paper, paper taken secretly from the store room at school, but I didn't feel particularly guilty because I was putting it to good use. Besides it wasn't that much paper, not really. In between the papers, I placed fashions I cut from my magazines—drawings of beautiful ladies in all types of clever shoes, darling skirts, silk blouses, and cunning hats. I also cut out agreeable looking children—the girls in drop waist smocks and dresses, the boys in short trousers and jackets of all sorts of patterns. I cut them very, *very* carefully and in this way of collecting, I learned to know what was *fine* and what was *poor*, what was *good* and what was *common*. This is what Myrtle calls *developing an eye for fashion*—and you will find that once *that eye* opens, it cannot be closed no matter what it has to look at. I wouldn't say it's a *burden*, exactly, but Myrtle probably would. Myrtle is *a martyr to fashion*.

Now, it wasn't just the drawings I collected. I cut out the best articles, too, and I practised reading them aloud—in English, of course—and getting my words just right—in case I should be called to read or speak in front of a crowd, or make an appearance in any sort of way. I stood in front of the little mirror in our girls' bedroom and elocuted with care. Proper elocution will open doors.

Once we had a family visiting on holiday from Kensington, which in case you don't know, has the best way of speaking in London. They had holdings in the quarry and came to check on it and visit with father. They walked around our town for a while, visiting Jones's shop, talking to him like they were old friends.

Parading about with utmost posture. I memorised the way they spoke—and walked—and practiced whenever I could, and I do believe I had developed the voice well. I practised it in my daily talking to anyone I encountered, something which seemed to annoy some of my classmates, my sisters, and my mother. Though I could not have cared less.

By the time I was fifteen years old, my keeping-box was nearly full of clippings, but I reckoned I still had two or three years before I could pack it all into a steamer trunk and head for London, with or *without* Father's permission. Most likely without. It's why I'd probably have no choice but to run away in the night.

In ladies' fashion the most beautiful gowns are made of fine wool and silk, my favourite is *taffeta*, which comes from the east. I'd never touched a real piece of taffeta, but I felt I knew the feel of it between my fingers having so admired drawings and descriptions. Taffeta is obviously very fine cloth, but even the *wool* in my magazines looked especially fine. It came in fuchsia and in lime green. And there were velvet-covered buttons on things, and even *darling* swimming outfits for days at the strand, just darling. Here, hardly anyone goes into the water without a boat under them.

Mother said, more than once, that I was showing signs of becoming an empty-headed snob, but it was only because she thought she'd seen me turning up my nose at *her* in her plain skirt and blouse. But I'm not as disrespectful as that. I assure you. And I assured her, too. That it never was *people* I turned my nose up at, just poorly made *things*. It wasn't her fault that all she could get here was less than she deserved. I tried to explain that everyone deserves fashion as nice as they have in London or Paris or New York City. Though I suppose I didn't really mean it, because it would grind my teeth to see some of my neighbours grumping along in such beautiful things and ruining them. They wouldn't take proper care of delicate fabrics, would they? They'd step all over the hems. She peered at me and said, 'Here, take this plate of oat cakes to your father for his tea, and don't knock your big head off on the doorway as you go through.'

'Yes, Mother,' I said with my eyes down. But on the inside I was thinking *it won't be soon enough that I'm well out of here. It won't be soon enough that I'm done carrying oatcakes and tiptoeing on eggshells to placate people who will never understand me.* Oh, I imagined the day that someone would be bringing scones to me on a little tray as I wrote my clever fashion pieces. As I imagined, I ate one of Father's oat cakes on the way to him in his chair because thinking about the future made me peckish. But he just chuckled when he saw me brushing the crumbs from my blouse. At that time, Father was often kind to me, unlike Mother.

I always shared a room with my sisters: Eirlys and Rhosyn.* My mother had named us each after a flower; how *gauche* I often thought. My sisters and everyone else, too, knew how I planned on going to London, having my life as a fashion writer, dressing very well as I've already told you. And maybe even becoming a *suffragette,* which was something I'd begun to think I might feel compelled to do once I got there. But they laughed and said *right to my face* that they thought I would grow out of such silly ideas, marry a local man, plain as the rest, and remain here forever just like them. Like all of them. And, besides, they said, suffragettes had left off since the war started. They'd said London was no place to be as you might be killed by a German Zeppelin at any moment.

Mother said this village life had been good enough for her family for as long as anyone could remember and why shouldn't it be good enough for me. Father said his family had left London behind. Left London and all its rats and smoke and came here grandfathers and grandfathers ago. He said it would be daft for me

---

*   Snowdrop and Rose

to go back. He looked my mother in the eye and winked. He said to her, 'Don't worry Mother, she will come to her senses. What's for tea?'

Only my sister Rhosyn ever understood that my intentions were real. She asked me, when I did get to London, might she join me after I'd settled in? Of course, I said yes, yes, but *only* on the condition that she take a new name for herself—I could not possibly *bear* to be a Lili living with another flower name in *public*. I suggested she select Elizabeth—or Simone, if she liked a French flair. She said perhaps I should change *my* name instead. I had to explain to her that since it was all my idea and I was the eldest sister, we would go by my rules. She rolled her eyes and laughed.

One damp, cold afternoon, I was on my way out the door of the Afar Shoppe with a new packet of old fashion magazines under one arm and a paper twist of wine gums in my free hand—which I'd bought earlier from Candaner's Sweet Shop. That's when Mr. Twm Gethin—who the locals call Twm Geth—fell into step beside me in his long coat and heavy clogs. Mr Gethin was uncouth at best, and people didn't like him in general. But I was not the snob my mother took me for, and I greeted him graciously.

'Good Day, Mr. Gethin. How are you this fine afternoon?' I'd learned all about proper salutation from the manners columns.

'Hello girl, might I have one of those gums, there?' Twm Gethin said, as if he were my school chum and we were strolling home from school. It was odd—the way he asked just as if he was a young boy though he was quite old. At least forty and maybe more, I reckoned. He held his palm out, and so I gave him two because it seemed miserly to hand over just one. Mind you, I only had about ten in all.

Regarding the wine gums, it was truly unusual for me to spend money on sweets as I was putting every coin I could find into a secret cup I'd hidden under our girls' bed—inside an old hat box—for my trip to London. Father was stingy and unyielding despite his position in management at the quarry, and he refused anyone but my mother an allowance, so it was a penny here and there but hardly anything. My savings cup wasn't even a quarter of the way full.

But when I'd found a penny, kicked up by the toe of my shoe in the muddy road, I'd been surprised, and so I bent down to have it, and slipped it into my pocket and went directly to Candaner's Sweet Shop for a treat. Despite my pressing need for savings. I'd been peckish for wine gums for weeks.

I KEPT WALKING AND didn't look at him to see if he was enjoying his wine gums, or if he would like another because I was not sure what else I should say to him after the initial greetings. I knew him only as tall Lowri Gethin's father—and the father of the Gethin boys as well—but though I'd seen the entire family in chapel every Sunday, I'd never spoken with the man in my whole life. I expected him to say thank you for the sweet and to go on his way down to the pub or else into a shop.

But, instead, he asked, 'What's there in that package, girl?'
'Oh, Magazines.'
'What *sort*?'
'Fashion Magazines'
'From where?' he asked, straightening his creased collar.
'London and America. And Paris.'
He asked me why I had them and about the fashions and the shoes and the lace and wool, and before I knew it I'd told him about how much I admired taffeta as well as my plan for life in London, right there walking up the village road, it just poured right out of me. And I thought it was nice to have someone ask,

but then, I soon felt I'd said too much and made a fool of myself, and so I resolved to say no more.

'London, girl. I have always wanted to move away to London myself. Truly. But there was no getting out of this place for me.'

His footsteps sounded mournful against the road, and I let his failure rest like a fog in my brain.

'You know,' he added slowly, 'you won't be let go so easy from Nefin, either. They'll say you think you're better than the rest, that you're putting on airs, and so, they'll do everything to make you stay.'

'I'm *not* putting on airs,' I protested, in spite of having promised myself to say no more, for what does one *do* to end a conversation with another person's father who persists in talking? 'I'm just *mad for fashion* is all.'

Mr. Gethin said that the newish brown wool skirt I had on that day, and my blouse with its collar and cuffs were better than any he'd seen here and that surely I was ready for London if London were ready for me. I was not sure what that meant, but it sounded powerful, and I assured him London was ready.

I had another wine gum and held out a third to him as well. 'Might as well, he announced as we rounded the bend, 'here's my cart and mule. Let me give you a lift home—I know where you Morgans live.' He winked when he said it and looked friendlier than my own father ever did.

I looked down at my lovely lace cuffs and smoothed them. It *was* beginning to rain, and it was a long walk home, so I accepted his offer with thanks. I gulped down the last wine gum—purple— and sprung up on the bench. As his young mule wrenched the wheels along the rutted road. The true rain seemed to hold itself off and so I broke my own rule about saving my magazines for home, and opened the packet halfway, peering in and still managing to keep the mist from wetting them. I enjoyed them while I travelled, and Mr. Gethin looked over and commented on the styles as he drove. He didn't know what they were called, and he couldn't see them well with how I was holding the pages, and with having to keep his eyes on the road, but he liked them. All.

He said he was sure I would look nice in most of the fashions which was no lie. I was soon lost in imagining a slightly older version of myself drifting through London—lavender summer-silk gown with a violet bodice complemented by pearl earbobs and cunning white boots—when I noticed Mr. Gethin was driving the cart through the forest on the wrong side of the old sawmill.

This was not the way to my house at all. And it was late afternoon with what little sign of the sun pushed itself through the mist dropping to the west. Mother would wonder where I was, and she was very strict about being home for supper on time. If I was late, she would be standing by the table waiting with a wooden spoon in hand, her face hard as a walnut.

Maybe Mr. Gethin was taking me to his house first so that Lowri could sit with me in the cart, even though we weren't close friends. But he wouldn't know that probably. I wondered, so I asked him outright if we were going to get Lowri, and he said no.

Nothing else.

Just 'No.'

He looked strange in the eyebrows.

He stopped talking to me about fashion.

He stopped talking entirely.

I reached into my bag to offer him another gum but then remembered I'd eaten the last one.

'Lili,' he finally said, 'I'm thinking there may be *some way* I can help you get to London. My old dat, when he was alive, he knew some men in London, important men. It *could be* they would help you with making connections—to the magazine editors and other people like that. I could write them a letter.'

We rounded a steep corner into the woods.

'But you mustn't tell anyone,' he continued, 'because if you *do*, then the whole of this place will want me to do favours for them as well. What do you think?'

I nodded. But I wanted to leave the cart. And he was slowing it down. The mule fought to keep moving and get his dinner at home and so Twm Gethin gave the reins a wrench back to make it stop. I wondered if I should jump out, but I felt it might be silly and rude to do so.

So I stayed put.

'You'll want to go to London, and the sooner the better or else you'll be trapped here. Married away to some soot-face or dust-face. You're old enough now. To be married. Aren't you? *Old enough*, I'd say, yes, Miss, you are.'

He took the magazines from my lap and set them neatly on the floorboard, and then he pushed his face against my neck, gritty with whiskers.

I wriggled away and he caught me fast. He said things, bad things, and pulled at my blouse buttons. I sat still, like a manikin, and he removed my blouse and lifted my skirt to my waist. More terrible words.

The damp air was cold on my skin. I made almost no noise when he spun me around and pushed me on my belly over the seat, no noise. It was just like in bad dreams, where you can't find your voice, and when you do, no air will fill your lungs at all.

Mr. Twm Gethin held my back down, pushing my belly so hard against the wood that I could barely breathe and then he stabbed me with that burning hot stab. I heard the mule snort and stomp at the front of the cart.

I knew what he was doing, of course, I wasn't completely ignorant. I cannot say if he held me there for minutes or hours, but when he let me go, he straightened my things, put my blue blouse right, buttoned it, and smiled with half of his mouth.

He lifted me back up to the seat and set me on it with a sickening gentleness.

He placed the magazines back in my lap, neatly.

'Let's get you home now,' he said, 'and don't forget what I said about London—these will be our secrets, just yours and mine.' I heard him say something *like that*, I'm sure, but I could no longer listen carefully. The words sounded like nonsense rumbling by. My head nodded on my neck, but not one word came from my mouth. It took all my strength to keep from vomiting all the wine gums I'd eaten into my lap.

Twm Gethin did not pull his cart all the way up our drive; instead, he stopped a distance from the house. He put one finger to his lip, and with the other hand he pointed to my magazines.

Like a thing hewn of wood, I dropped down from the cart and walked stiffly to the house with the mule's clopping fading away behind my back.

I went quietly to our girls' bedroom where I told Rhosyn—who was sprawled across our bed reading her new Jack London book about a wolf—that I felt I might be coming down with a fever, and contagious. A warm wash would be just the thing. I knew she hated to be interrupted when reading, but she was a fine sister and so she brought me a pitcher of hot water from the stove, a fresh dress from the wardrobe, and a bar of Pears soap, with which I scrubbed myself silently behind our privacy curtain in the room's corner.

She was back to her book already.

When I came in to supper, freshly dressed, Mother asked why I'd been late home

I told her it was just the threat of rain that held me up.

I tried several times to say more—my mouth opened to say the words, but nothing would come out. For surely, she would tell Father, and then I would be *ruined*—ruined like the poor simple girl up the hill whom no one would speak to, and who walked far behind the rest of her family when they went to church. And not just ruined, worse. To have them know what Mr. Gethin had done to me would be *humiliating*. I just couldn't.

And worse yet, if he knew, I imagined Father would take an axe and ride up to the Gethin house to *hack* Twm Gethin to pieces. But no, surely, Twm Gethin—being larger and stronger than Father— would snatch the axe from Father and would hack *Father* to pieces instead. Father was an office man whose people had little experience in such things. Father wore a monocle. People who wear monocles are not good at fisticuffs.

And if Father survived it, I'd have to live with his judgement. Why did I ever get into that cart with Twm Gethin he'd want to know, with Twm Gethin of all people. Twm Gethin whom Father named weekly over tea as 'an eternally vexing fly in the ointment, always causing trouble at the mine, a damnable buzzing insect—a Geth-fly!'

I washed myself six or seven more times that night, with the rough cloth, winnowing the soap to nearly nothing, until I was completely red raw. And I hung my skirt and blouse to the very back of the wardrobe. I laid my magazines in the corner, and there they remained. But I did not drop my dream. I wanted to go to London more than ever now, to leave this place and never ever return.

It was my terrible misfortune that I missed my courses. And soon my belly grew. It began with a tiny hard little lump down low and a constant tingling up above. But I still couldn't tell *anyone*. Not even my sisters. Sometimes it was there, ready to pop out of my mouth like a soap bubble, but it never did. I was always relieved that it didn't, for a moment, and then terrified again for as Father always says, 'In time, everything will out.'

On Sundays, I prayed in chapel for God to *move* the child from me to someone who wanted one, maybe even Aderwen Gethin, the wife of Twm Gethin. Yes, *that* would have solved things. I reckoned that if God could perform miracles then perhaps, if I prayed hard enough, he would do just this one for me. And if he did, I'd never ask for anything again.

Every night, I waited until my sisters left our bedroom before undressing and washing as I grew and grew and grew. I took a scissor and needle and thread to move the hooks on my skirts. Mornings, I gagged on the smell of rashers and at the fumes of Father's pipe. I lived in fear at school and at home because it's very hard to keep such a secret—it's hard to keep and it's hard to know it must end without knowing how or when.

It seemed to me that I *must* go to London before anyone found out, far ahead of plan, but I certainly didn't have enough money. My savings cup was pitifully low on savings. So, I began searching Father's waistcoats for coins, and I took almost half of Mother's pin money when she wasn't looking, and I let her accuse Rhosyn of having stolen it for sweets without ever confessing it was me. Even when Rhosyn was being slapped about, I kept quiet. I told myself how Rhosyn was *always* taking pennies for sweets without being caught, so it wasn't altogether wrong.

I even devised a plan to offer to help Mr. Jones with the shop so that he could have the day off and take the entire load from his cash drawer and then flee. But Mr. Jones said he didn't need a shop clerk, and thank you very much, but he preferred to be in the shop than anywhere else these days.

I truly did everything to find money except to go to Twm Gethin. I suppose a craftier girl might have demanded some money from him, but I couldn't bring myself to it. Oh, no, quite the opposite; I peered and peeped constantly to avoid any sight of him. I skulked from home to school and back each day, but I couldn't get my schoolwork done because I was so very tired. My sisters had to help me with it even though they were younger than me, but they didn't mind.

I was so very tired for months. Though at least while I slept I hadn't any feeling of panic. Mother didn't like the pallor in my face, so she fed me cod liver oil twice a day to cure the low blood she was certain plagued me. I swallowed the oil without complaint and then politely excused myself to vomit it up behind the crack willow near the stream behind our house. Its springtime catkins hid me like a curtain, its pollen dust fell, yellowing my pointed boots and I stayed there for as long as I could.

One evening as I was undressing for bed, Eirlys came rushing in to say Mother had made a custard with berries, which was her favourite and mine, and I should come to the table for it now. But I was caught by surprise and my sister saw me standing there in the light from the lamp, my nightgown in hand, my belly taut and misshapen as an egg—my hair hiding my breasts but reaching only the top of my rounded middle. She might have stared for a while before I noticed her, and the expression on her face was shock.

'Don't!' I pleaded, but she ran for Mother, yelling, 'Lili's got the bloat! Like a sick cow! She's *enormous!*'

Mother came and took a long look, stood stock still for a few minutes, and then went for Father. I would not let Father see my belly, but there was no need, it was now evident behind my skirt. Everyone was shouting. My sisters in wordless screams and my parents in pointed sentences. What Mother and Father shouted were not oaths but questions. I did not answer. Just stood there crying with relief and fear and shame, mainly shame, because their questions held no softness, no care, only judgement.

The questioning went on for hours, until in exhaustion and frustration they started a chorus to accuse Mr. Jones because he was the only man they were aware I had any traffic with. And poor Mr. Jones already had too much to deal with. So that's when I told them the one thing I should never have said and said it only out of desperation, imagining them trotting down to accuse the old shopkeeper. I said *Twm Gethin*. Which was, of course, the truth.

'Twm Geth!' That was Father, bellowing like a trumpet. 'What were you doing with *Twm Geth* of all people?'

As he shouted, he spluttered and wrestled his own arms, which were rioting against him, into his jacket. His plan was written all over his face—to storm to the pub. He shouted through the open door as he left home, 'Geth, that blackguard, is sure to be there!'

Mother, her face flushed and her hands in hard little fists, paced the floor and shooed my sisters out of the room. I could see she was willing them to un-see what they had seen, me as I had become. Her breathing was fast and she trotted the flagstone floor. She made it known she couldn't bear to look at me by not looking at me, and for that I was glad. I didn't know if I should sit in a chair or go to my room. So, I stood there. Mother paused in her pacing only to chase out my sisters as they trotted in again and again, staring, one and then the other, and then both together, knowing such a thing could happen to them but also knowing that it had *not*. That it had happened to *me*.

I continued to cry, having fully given up respectable restraint, and soon found that I could not stop at all. My eyes swelled shut and my nose closed so completely that had someone put their hand over my mouth, I would have suffocated to death.

My mother paced back and forth, back and forth. I wanted her to take me into her arms, or, better yet, to run out after my father and stop him from any fatal foolishness. She did neither.

Soon enough, and shockingly, Mr. Gethin stood in our kitchen, in one piece and looking quite healthy—his cowlick up like a rooster's comb. I listened to him and Mother and Father speak in short, choppy sentences. Mother mainly said, 'Oh, my Lord!' Father mainly said 'Something's got to be done, Geth!' and Mr. Gethin made agreeing sorts of noises. I was in the room, but no one talked to *me*. This went on for some time, until Mr. Gethin suggested I be sent to Cardiff. He said that Father with his big office job should be able to afford the expense.

'They have homes for *such girls* in such places as Cardiff,' he added.

And then, finding no one speaking over him, Mr. Gethin continued: 'That's the best thing to do if you ask me, and then the child can go into the orphanage, and *this one* can come back home, no one the wiser. Cardiff is so full of all sorts of people; she wouldn't be noticed there at all.'

'I'm not *asking* the likes of you,' Father said as he glared at Gethin who'd stopped to admire my mother's ironware butter dish as if he were in Jones's shop, 'I'll have you *know* you are responsible here! And since you have contributed to this problem, you can contribute to a solution, in sterling as well as words. My daughter is *ruined*. And I'll not have her sisters dragged through the mud as well.' Mr. Gethin replied with a strange kind of confidence that seemed to come from seeing I wasn't going to tell how he pushed me down against my will.

'Yes then,' he announced, 'it's got to be Cardiff; she was after going to London all the while anyhow, wasn't she? She wants to get out into the world—*some girls do*—but she'll have to behave herself there, won't she?'

Father twitched like a terrier, but Mother pulled him back down by his coat sleeve.

'It'll do no good to be angry at this point, George.'

She'd suddenly become the voice of reason, seeing a way out of it all and was ready to make arrangements. She had two other daughters to think of, and herself to boot, so she saved everyone but *me*.

'True,' said Mr.Gethin, 'I'm an *honest* man, and I never tell a lie. I've got to say, George, I shouldn't have done it, but I'm simply a man, and aren't all men tempted by sin? All I can do is confess to God and help you people, and I confessed long ago, weeks and weeks ago, so all that's left to do is help.'

I think Father must have known I wasn't willing, that I wasn't really a bad girl; I think that's why he rose as he did before Mother stopped him, but the thing is, it didn't matter, willing or not, there I was, in a predicament and with no way to be forgiven. By God, yes, perhaps, but by people, never. Of course, Twm Gethin was 'responsible' as Father had said, but he, himself, was not in any real predicament, not compared to me, and to accuse him in the town would only bring shame on my own family—we all knew this, particularly my sisters who peeped out from the back bedroom. It didn't matter that Father was more respected than nearly any man in the quarry or that Gethin was a fly in the ointment; none of that mattered in the least any more.

When the adults quieted down for a moment, I tried to say that I wasn't feeling up to travel just yet, that perhaps London was a better choice than Cardiff, that maybe I could keep the baby. Maybe I could find work, as a nanny or such, or maybe even in the fashion houses, where there were all sorts of modern women with unknown and mysterious pasts. I'd read about such things. But I hadn't gotten past the first two words when I was told to *shut up* by all three. My mother held her fingertips to her temples, which meant she had a sick headache coming on.

'*You*,' Father said, shoving a chair under the table for emphasis, 'will think of your sisters and of this family and of your God above. You will have this child, give it up, and come back to this house to be a dutiful daughter until such time as it is possible to find you a husband, if it is possible at all. You will *never* speak of this to anyone, and neither will your sisters.' His monocle fell out from his eye as he twitched at me.

Over the next few weeks those three made arrangements for me to travel: True to his word, Mr. Twm Gethin booked the train ticket to Cardiff and sent a note to Father to say he'd found a place for me in a House of Mercy there. Mother suddenly was against it and put forth that I should stay hidden in the house, here where we stand now. 'Why move her away to Cardiff?'

'Because,' explained Father with some impatience, 'then there's no chance of anyone finding out, and the child can be put for adoption immediately, far from *this family*!' Mother nodded, and I do think that was her last moment of say-so gone.

She let out the waists of my skirts properly, packed my things into a small trunk and removed me from the school roster, telling the headmaster I was going to tend to a sick aunt in Glamorgan. The headmaster said, it's for the best; she's more educated than she need be already. We had no relatives in Glamorgan, of course.

My sisters flitted like shadows away from me, as if I *indeed* had something contagious. I began to soothe myself with thoughts of Cardiff at Christmastide, as Christmas *was* coming—of ladies skating in fur trimmed skirts, or musicians on street corners and roasted nuts, as there might be in Cardiff, for wasn't it a *real city* like London?

And surely, I'd get there in time to see it all. Even better, there'd be other girls like me to talk to. Girls who wouldn't press themselves to the walls for fear of my brushing past them, me a shameful thing. And when it was all over, I'd come back here like father said, but only for a short time. Once I had my strength back and some money saved, I'd be off to London in the dead of night.

And I'd make my fortune there—away from all their punishments and shame. I *would*!

But their carefully crafted plans for The House of Mercy at Christmastide in Cardiff came to nothing when my pains began two nights before I was to leave—nearly a month before my time. At first, they were not very bad, and I thought I might deliver a child as easily as a cat or a cow does—or as even as easily as Dilys Powell down the road, who is famous for her fourteen children and none of them having required more time-off than an afternoon, but I was mistaken. My labour would be long.

My MOTHER IS MY midwife—to keep it all a secret—and she tends to me for hours, and then for days as the pains build on one another. She's short with me, and even though she holds my hand, she doesn't look at my face. She keeps her knees together and sits upright in the chair beside my bed, reminding me not to hold my breath, and more importantly, reminding me that I've brought this pain upon *myself*. I might be glad when it's over, but I best strive to never forget it. Keep it as a reminder, she says with her eyes looking toward the window no one can see out, the dark curtains drawn tight.

It goes on and on and on, and I swallow my pain, not wanting to give her the satisfaction of hearing it, for as long as I can. But then, it simply rips through me head to toe. That's when Mother finally sends Rhosyn to get the *real* midwives.

Marged Dafydd comes in, with her granddaughter close by her side, and they smell of dark herbs. I cannot see them, but that smell and the sound of the old woman's deep voice make me think they will help me and they will save me. The old woman comes in close to the bed and pushes Mother away, 'Why did you wait *so long?* When the girl's this young I need to be fetched early, not late!' She bristles, moving the air and muttering about foolish, foolish people.

I vomit over the side of the bed.

the old woman doesn't mean to scare me, I know it by the way she tells the younger one to rub my back and smooth my hair, but the pain, the pain, the pain. I don't care anymore who's kind and who's vicious. I only want the pain to stop. I only want this part of things to be over and done.

'A foot,' I hear Mother, and it sounds as if she's underwater. Hands push blanket after blanket under me and pull them away again soaked. The midwife is hurting me more. I shiver so hard my front tooth chips and I feel the chip against my tongue, but I can't stop shivering.

I'm so cold.

Only the blood between my legs is warm—and only when it gushes.

I hear the midwife's granddaughter crying, and I wonder how to thank her for crying for me. But I can't make a word.

No, I can't talk over the screaming that jumps up from my own lungs.

I'm not frightened of death itself—not really.

It's something else about dying that's so terrible.

It's about dying *now*.

Pain is breaking my body and it's certain I will *never* get to London.

Never

Not even as far as Cardiff.

The Gravity of Foresight

Marged Dafydd • 1845-1920

I loved most the smell of lavender and rosemary, crushed and mixed well. This, with a cloud of burning sage, will cleanse any room or body until it is pure and new as the new day. You should also know that the juice of a snail dripped directly in from above will cure ailments of the eyes, but it's best to make a broth for sipping as well and take these cures together when the moon is dark. Listen to me carefully, because I am unsure that a healer can still exist in Cymru as once was the case. Even in my lifetime there were fewer and fewer of us, and so I tell secrets now, secrets I would not have told you in my life. I was stricter then. More wedded to secrecy. As has always been necessary for wise women, midwives, healers—those who might be called witches by certain others. The secrecy was always to preserve the knowledge and to preserve our lives. But things have changed. There are new midwives, I hear, regulated midwives. We are not them.

Listen now, you must not rely on this doctor in town, any of these doctors, with their cutting and cutting off. They have no respect for the ways of nature and work against everything they encounter rather than with. They battle rather than heal—they call it healing—but it is only a sort of fighting. I taught all of my lore, this and more, to my granddaughter, but I foresaw clearly that she would not have children and so I know it will have been lost with her by now, so you must listen. All of you who pass by must listen as if you were my shadow's apprentice. For surely you had an old *nain** of your own, once, and know how to listen.

My granddaughter, who was also called Marged like me, was always after me to write it all down, but I would not, though I could write a little. I had learned from the school teacher in return for treatments. The old midwives in the other valleys cannot write, but they can speak as I do, well and steadfast in healing and delivering. All midwives and cunning folk understand the power of words, and whether in Welsh or some other language—even in English—they hold power. As I must speak for you now, I will measure each word with care. We do not write down things that should be summoned by and stored in the mind or pulled from the river of knowledge. All words are part incantation when they come from the tongue.

I let my granddaughter Marged think I could not read nor write at all because I had to teach her that a healer must hold it all in her head. Some may call that a lie. I do not.

I learned healing and proper mourning from my father's father, my *taid,*** and he from his own grandfather, a wise man— *Dyn Hysbys,**** surely you have heard of them—and so on in an unbroken thread snaking back to places so old and long ago that we can remember only the taste of them. But it is in this way that the natural things of the forest and meadow, of rock and fire and

---

*   Grandmother
**   Grandfather
***   Ancient wizards, cunning folk, leads back to the Druids

water, impart their wisdom again and again. That is the chain of healing; perhaps you, too, are part of it. Perhaps that is why you have been sent my way.

Like most healers, I had the second sight, even as a child, and so did my old *taid*, father of my father, who taught me the leaves and roots and magic words in this very little cottage, here, what's left of it. I can see as well as you can that it's in ruins, but see how the thresholds have held. They are made of elm.

Here, in this place, *Taid* also taught me to beat rhythm on the *tabwrdd* and blow the pipe. I'll call it tabor so you may understand, in case you've little or no Welsh. Or should I say *drum*? One instrument under my arm and the other upon my lips was strong medicine, and I could bring sleep, trance, transition or liveliness to any body with my music. And because of this I had always to take great care when passing by the hollows and hills of the *Tylwyth Teg,** for the fair folk will cause a musician to stay and stay with them forever. I respect them, but had no wish to stay in their spell. It's not for us.

Besides music and healing, I was trained well in old midwifery, which is special, on its own. Set apart. This, from my *nain*, for only a woman can know the craft. She let me practise, in my childhood, on her own three ewes. She said ewes are not so different from most women in such ways—no, nor are cows. These both can find themselves in dire straits at the birth and need a helping hand, so you might as well be there if you can. But some animals, she said, cats for instance, have no trouble at all. A cat wants no help with birthing. Some women, she said, are like cats, but they are rare and hearing tell of them can give other women false confidence. What I learned in my own time is that while most women might be like sheep and there is always the possibility of trouble in birthing,

---

*   Fair family or fair folk/faeries often mischievous or potentially dangerous

lambs are not like babis, not with those long hooved legs kicking out ahead of them to pull on. Nor are rams like men. Rams do not stand at the door pacing and sweating, nor do they mourn when the lamb or the ewe is lost. Thus, my practising with sheep was limited useful, and when I turned about twelve, my nain began to take me from house to house to witness our neighbour women labouring, just like I would later take my own granddaughter Marged, letting her see it all; from the fat and happy births of the Priddy children to the poor Morgan girl, nothing but agony to the end.

Oh, I knew where it was headed when I saw her rounding face in the Morgan window one midnight as I passed by—a three-month before she went—when no one but me, and me only just then, knew she was with child. In the moment I saw her light the candle there, I knew she would not survive it. It was plain in my sight. The sight is not a blessing but a precious burden, like raising a grandchild when you are tired already. Exhausting and yet a gift of great proportion. And though I knew she would die, I helped her as best I could. The sight doesn't mean you get to stand back. And you never do know when destiny might change its winds. Though that's rarer than rare in my knowing.

My own taid and nain lived to be some of the oldest people anyone knew, and I watched them carefully as they were knowers of all things. They went about together with their little wizened heads like shrunken apples, leaning toward one another. They said it was because they each healed the other that they lived almost forever. They said they were past one hundred summers but who was counting. Then they laughed. For they had no end of merriment in them. In this they were different than me—I was always a serious one no matter how I tried to lighten myself. It was simply my nature.

Taid and Nain made their home in this cottage where they raised me, but even when I was young, they were seldom inside it. It was, to them, no more than a place to warm by the fire when the weather was truly grim and a spot to store their gatherings. They were of the sort who live mainly outdoors. Like the druids of tales and truth. Even if the weather was grey and raining, wrapped in layers of wool rubbed with sheep's oils, and with sacks on their backs, they went gathering and asking permission of the trees to gather firewood. Taid had another reason for wandering with Nain, one more important to him than any herb or mushroom they might find: he sought the unicorn, and he was certain it kept itself best in the rain, that it grazed on wettest grasses so that it need never approach a stream. He insisted that he must have Nain with him always so that when he finally spied it, she would spy it as well. He wouldn't want to see the wonderous creature without her seeing it, too. Nain went willingly as she'd been out in the mists and rain since forever. But I preferred to remain inside playing my tabor at the fireside, for I was in training for a healer and thought myself too big a girl to hunt unicorns with Taid and Nain anymore. I no longer believed they would find one. Besides, I didn't care for wet on my feet.

That spring, my mam and dat over at their place fell to the quick coughing sickness, as did my brothers and sisters—every last one—no matter that Taid mixed crushed snails and calf's lung water for them, or that Nain left hot oats with the sign of the cross in a cup by the casement. She murmured prayers and incantations day and night in both new and old religions, but still not a one was spared. We even stood two whole nights outside their door, chanting the Lord's Prayer along with many older things. But we daren't go inside, for there's no incantation stronger than the miasma when it's rolling. Nain said that, in the end, the cures didn't work because we could not get nutmeg, and nutmeg is the best cure, but there was none to be had as it comes from a long way off and we might see it only on rare occasion in those days. We had to wait for the ships from Ireland or some slow cart to cross from the south for any rare spice—and most of its wares sold long before it arrived here, remote as we were. And if some did arrive it was often too dear to have. If only there had been nutmeg.

In the year 1857, then, my whole family back at home was taken. And so, I was to stay with Taid and Nain forever more, without a visit or a cup of tea with a brother or sister, mother or father ever again. I threw myself into mourning with abandon, weaving a lopsided black wool shawl, which I then wore day and night over my head like a hood. I dyed my lips and fingertips with berry juice and darkened my eyelids with the dust of black clay thinned with spring water. I took to sighing instead of breathing and played only the most sorrowful lament I knew on my tabor and pipe until Nain said I could not come with her to any more births the way I was behaving. I'd cast a curse of sorrow on any child born in my presence. I might even harm the babi inside a woman should she cross my path with me in such a foul state. Besides, Nain said, it was selfishness. Had I forgotten that she'd lost her child and her grandchildren as well? Had I not thought perhaps I was making her pain greater?

'Keep it to your evening rituals and prayers,' she snapped to me. 'Stop yourself from this.'

But I could not stop it. I was caught up. And every day, when Nain and Taid went out of the house, I crept up to the tiny looking glass Nain kept in her wooden box. It was no larger than my hand. I set it on the table, leaned up against the clay pot of daisies Nain kept there in summer, and gazed at my mournful self. I watched how I cried, and the tears made my eyes even more blue, like bluebells, I thought. Quite fetching in a sad way. I was alive and beautiful and distraught. I watched my image in utter fascination. The sight of my sorrow made me cry the more. One afternoon I lingered long, backing up from the mirror and tying a green sash around my waist, accentuating its slimness and pulled in a stifled sob, imagining myself beautiful and piteous. I turned to the side and admired my beginning bosom, eyes still tearing.

I did not see the door swinging open its silent, well-greased hinge, nor did I see Nain, bent and tired from a night-long unsuccessful delivery, in which both mother and club-footed twins perished, dragging herself through the door. I did not see her at all until her hand swept out from beside me and sent the tiny looking glass flying against the stone wall. And then her other hand, barely behind the first one, slapped across my face with a crack like a horseman's whip.

'Enough!' she thundered, small as she was. 'Enough of this! Is this what you were at while Mare Lewis down the road and her two little babis were breathing their last? I needed your help! But you are unfit for human companionship. And instead, *this*? This! You great clot of selfishness!'

Now, Nain had never before shouted in my face, or in anyone's face as far as I knew. I looked down shamefully, the green sash dropping from my hand to the cool flag floor, my cheeks burning red. I kept my eyes down, but still I saw Taid standing silently in the doorway. He said nothing, not then, not for weeks to me. Nor did she. Her slap, though, stung my head for a very long time. I lived, ashamed, in the silence.

I picked up my looking glass and wrapped it in a bit of cloth. I put it away with my things in my chest. I was sadder than ever before, and I had met real shame and learned its flavour. But, because I felt contrary and bristled at the thought of making apology, two moons passed before I approached Nain to say I was sorry and would change my ways. I promised her, and myself, that I would not keep a looking glass about my person ever again. I hoped she'd say I might, in time, and undo my vow right there, but no, she did not. She looked me in the eye.

'You had best not, girl, for a looking glass is danger to *you*; you are the sort it splits into two. This is your weakness. Don't ever forget it or others will pay for your forgetfulness.'

I had not the heart to play my tabor and pipe for some time and dragged myself around the place, shuffling my feet and sighing and wondering if I looked as cast down as I felt.

I'll confess I did catch glimpses of myself in the pool down in the valley, and in the gleam of other people's eyes if the light was right, so I did know my looks, but only very vaguely, in that watery way. Such a wilful girl, I was. But I did keep my vow, and even on my wedding day, as I arranged and rearranged my myrtle bouquet, I dared not ask for a looking glass. Dylan thought me the most humble and modest of women, one who never looked at herself; he did not know my reason then. More the fool, him. But years later, when we lay in our bed, four children already born, I confessed my early vanity to him, and he only laughed at me. And not at all unkindly. When he stopped, he offered to buy me a good oval glass to hang just inside the door, when he got rich, which he never would, but I said no, no, Nain was right about me.

Nain and Taid were long gone by the time Dylan offered me the looking glass, but I still felt them about me, as if they were tucked away under my two shoulder blades. This is the way it is with the dear ones if you sit still for them and take them along with you.

Nain and Taid had gone out to collect the red mushrooms, red speckled flies, and they never came back. Dylan searched for them, but he could not find them. I searched as well, afraid of what might be found, but I found nothing. I looked down wells and under fallen oaks. I called out like a curlew and like a gull until my throat burned. The strangest thing was that Taid's own tabor and pipe were missing. He always kept them wrapped in a tansy-yellow blanket and put them up in the wall away from the heat of the hearth and the cold of the door. I lived the rest of my life feeling that those ancient ones might swing open that silent door at any moment and step inside, a unicorn with them. I must say, I longed for their return. I longed for them despite my satisfaction with the companionship of my husband and later the company of my children, for there's a longing that comes to settle when you lose the last of those who knew you as a child. I put my own tabor and pipe into the cupboard, behind the babi blankets I kept there, and I vowed that when Taid came back, I'd play again with him. I'm still waiting, even now. Even though it's clear they live only under my shoulders, a layer down and nearer to the mountain.

I was left to do all the healing and all the midwifing for the entire area and a bit beyond. I'd been trained well by my nain, and with her and him gone, I was no longer a vain girl but a serious woman overnight though I was only twenty years old. My man Dylan was a smallholder with some arable land but no house. I was a woman with a cottage of her own now, but no farm fields to speak of, so we lived in my house and he farmed his fields, growing mainly swedes, which he sold at market and which I boiled and mashed for our suppers with a knob of butter to top it. Our cow was a healthy one, and we had a few sheep as well that had come down from Nain's ewes. We did this happily. We had children and seldom a cross word between us. I do not like to talk over it too much and lessen the magic of what's simple. Dylan helped me to gather when he could. He swallowed and tested my medicines and carried my gathering bags for near twenty years. Which was not long enough to suit me, but I'd foreseen it and was not surprised. When my Dylan died, planting swedes on a Saturday afternoon, I learned to mourn yet again—in earnest and unending. And even now, I am still here thinking of my good man who must be somewhere very nearby.

When all of my children had gone out into the world, boys to the quarry, girls into marriage, my husband already up in the graveyard, I found myself alone and lonely, so I took in my namesake Marged—my eldest granddaughter—to teach. I was her nain, her *nain*, but she insisted on calling me Gran, which made me frown. As you know, words being magic, something like the name by which you are called is so very important. And to my mind, it's best to stay close to the Welsh when it's important like that. But she learned that English word from her mother before I got her. But I let her say it because she smiled when she did and she was still small and tender when she came to me. It's surprising the things you allow your grandchildren that you would shake out of your children.

Though I knew with clear vision that Marged would have no children, I despaired of that nonetheless, for it meant our craft would end with her, at least in this valley and the four hills surrounding. The doctors with their black bags and black boot-shoes were taking over. Even in the case of birthing, which turned my blood cold. We had to keep the art going. Keep it between women where it belonged. I suggested that Marged find a learner from another town, maybe an orphan—god knows there are plenty of orphans in the countryside between the consumption and the typhoid— but she did not. I had once considered taking up Lili Morgan's babe, but I was shown it was not her destiny, no matter how much I wanted it to be. You cannot bend destiny and when you try, it swings back like an iron gate and knocks things into disarray.

I never wanted to tell my granddaughter she wouldn't ever have a child of her own, that I'd known from early on in her courses. Seen the hollowness in her womb. It was not a needful thing for her to know until she knew it for herself. What's more, her barrenness was the sort that draws life to it, and that would make her a more tender healer, so in truth, I never doubted my choice in Marged as my learner, but I did worry so about who would carry on after her.

I lived as long as I could in order to teach her everything I knew, but not so long as not to allow her her own time to flourish. The foxglove had been keeping me for some time, but even that has its limits. The heart, you know. I recognised its troubles and treated myself. And when I was satisfied with things as they were, I stopped taking it. And I died without much pain, but then again, I knew how to do that. We cannot bend destiny, but we can walk alongside it in our own way.

What I want to know is will you stay and learn? Learn something from me. Have you got an ink pen and paper? Pencil? I'll allow it, now, so that you won't forget what I say. Allow writing my knowings. Here's what you need to know first—our first lesson begins now.

The mountain air is full of health and the marsh air of sickness. If you come across a sick one living near the marsh, the first thing to do is wrap him in blankets and fetch two bearers to remove him to the mountain. There's a sick house there with a tiny hearth, and with a pass-through window for food. It's been there a very long time, but if you squint your eyes you will see it. The plank the sick one is moved on must be purified with burned sage and painted with blood of a lamb before you put him onto it. And take this down too now— the skin of a puppy should be wrapped over the man's left foot and the bearers should chant a special prayer the entire time they bear him:

Oh, God of the Mountain Air

Oh, God of the Forest
We will pilgrimage to the Isle of Saints
When this soul has had his cure
Oh, God, please cure this soul…

Now, say it in Welsh with me—I can teach you:

Oh, Dduw Gwynt y Mynydd
Oh, Dduw'r Goedwig
Awn ar bererindod i Ynys Enlli
Pan caiff yr enaid yma iachâd
Oh, Dduw, iachâd i'r enaid hwn y gweddïwn

If you practice every day, you will soon remember. You may sing it if you like. Welsh is the most natural of languages—some say it's the first one. God's very own. And I wouldn't disagree with those who say so.

Now, I know you have far to walk, for I can see that about you, and I see you are tired. It would take you the rest of your natural life to take down all I need to tell you. It cannot be done in this way tonight alone, but you've a good bit to take away and use for now. And it may be that if you listen for me, I can speak through distances to you. Do try to remember this, if nothing else: you may return to me, and if you do, I will tell you more. Bring your children if you have them.

The Ambivalence of Truth

Twm Gethin • 1870-1942

Twm Geth, here. Gethin if you want to say it proper. Steward at the quarry *and* a man with a prime small holding, no landlord hovering over me. Kind of steward gets to come into the main office—that kind. Began as a low-down cutter, just like most in the quarry. Made my way up and fast, too, which is most unusual. Too fast for the likes of some in the office, especially those who came from down south and such. Those who thought themselves better than us locals. But I never got full of myself or above myself. In fact, I made it my habit to have a pint with my friends any payday to show them that I was still one of them, always would be.

The most important thing about me is I was known all around these parts as an honest man. Never thought myself better than another man, never thought myself worse. And what's more and is most unusual, I can say I never told a lie, ever. And me saying so would be true! Now, I certainly have done some wrong in my life. To do some wrong is the option of every man so long as he atones for it later. No one is without sin; doesn't our lord say that?

He does, he does. But, rare as such truthfulness as mine may be, it's real as anything. I wouldn't bear false witness. What's more, there was never a man alive—no matter his size—could push me into telling a lie either. Though many a man—and woman—tried.

And that's just how I set the tone for my own children, too—not a single liar in the entire tribe of mine. And not many around here can say that. In fact, I've heard it said that the average person lies at least three times per day. Not us Gethins, though. And it's not just a small handful of children I raised to be upstanding characters, no, it's *seven*—and the youngest on my own after the wife quit us. Yes, it's a sad story to tell, that, but I'll tell it short. The wife—her name is Aderwen—now, she ran off the very day little Betsan came to us. Just packed her bag and out the door she flew. Never to return.

At first, I thought she was just blowing off steam out there stalking up and down the mountain, but I was wrong on that count. When she was gone overnight, I knew she wasn't coming back. I chalked it up to the madness that sometimes comes over women of a certain age, or of any age, if you know what I mean, though. Women are prone to hysteria, you know. And truth be told, Aderwen had been strange with me for some time—quiet and bitter. Long-faced. I'd thought maybe it was that I stayed too late in the pubs with my friends, or that our children were growing past needing mothering—that can make a woman feel pure useless. In fact, that sad uselessness and me feeling like cheering Aderwen out of it is partly why when old Marged Dafydd and her bristling bitch of a granddaughter crossed my path on the road early one cool morning as I was headed home from the pubs, and handed me a *babi bach** to take up to the orphanage, I thought to

---

*   Little baby

bring it home instead. Thought maybe Aderwen would see it and perk right up.

Like I said, the Dafydds didn't intend to give the babi to me in the least. They only wanted the helpless little thing taken up to the place on the far hill. The orphanage. In fact, at first, they refused to let me have her. They were all for me carrying her up the hill but not keeping her. Oh, they were used to giving orders around here, alright, these two. And the old one held out the willow basket to me like she was an empress of France or something.

'Take this babi to the orphanage,' she said with her hand on her hip, 'and you *best not* take it home to your woman; she doesn't need the strife, Gethin.' The young one, who always travelled along like a witch's familiar, pulled her beetle brows down into her very eyes at me. She held up her apron skirt all covered in blood like a butcher might. Then she waved it at me and the old one bellowed, 'Lili Morgan dead down the road, and it's the least *someone* could do to see this babi to safety. To the orphanage.' The little scrap mewled and squirmed in its swaddling, and the road was empty but for the four of us. The old one pointed right at me and said, 'You hear me, Geth? It's no more than a long walk to the orphanage, so here's the child, and get moving.'

Well. Those midwives might know midwifing, they *might*. But they didn't know me so well as they thought they did. And maybe they didn't even know midwifing as well as everyone thought. The fact that Lili Morgan was dead down the road didn't stand as any great proof of their skill, but either way, no surly pair of battle-axe midwives was going to order me around. Besides, I reckon a babi is always a blessing, no matter how it's gotten, even if it's found on the road or handed over by meddling midwives at dawn on your way home from the pub and you with a splitting headache. Why should little Betsan—I'd already named her by then—why should she languish in the orphanage? Wasn't Moses himself raised in an adopted home with no outside interference at all from midwives and their like? He was.

'Don't do it,' croaked the Dafydds, like they were reading my mind.

'I will,' I said.

'*Don't*,' they said again.

And so, I went off toward home with the bundle.

'Suit yourself,' the young one yelled at my back.

'I intend to!'

But my Aderwen refused the babi bach—oh yes, she did—and she splashed me in the face with dregs of tea for ever bringing it home. All in all, she went utterly mad, packed her bag, kicked the cat, and quit the place.

Like I said before, she never returned to us, but I always knew where she was, didn't I? Oh yes, I did. She was right up the hill with Agnes Monroe. Like a cat to the devil, she ran up there. To old pigeon-toed Aggie Monroe, who never did find herself a man in her whole entire life.

A handful of days later, after I told my friends Aderwen had left me, and they said that with our youngest boy turning fifteen and Aderwen thinking to herself she was in the clear, it must be that she just couldn't warm to the idea of raising a babi again. They said that's what *their wives* said, at least, when they'd told them of my situation—which I'd asked them specifically *not to do*. But friends don't listen when it comes to gossip. They're altogether worse than women. Blabbermouths, every one of them. I wasn't sure if they believed the babi had come from Aderwen herself or if they knew about the midwives. I just left it to itself.

Those wives had told them that the thought of rising in the night all over again is enough to send any woman trotting away when she thinks she's done with it since she's gone through the change herself. Just haven't got the *stamina* anymore, those wives said. Unlike a man, who can do his part up to the grave, their husbands had added.

Sometimes, my friends asked where, exactly, Aderwen had gone off to, like they'd forgotten what I said last time they asked, so I had to tell them again and again. I started to think they were just baiting me, but they wouldn't dare. Still, wasn't it plain to see with eyes in their heads? Surely the whole of the Nefin and every surrounding farmer had witnessed the ridiculous sight: Aderwen, with a lip on her so long it dragged the ground. Grim as the reaper himself picking beans in Aggie Monroe's garden. Up in spinster Aggie Monroe's paltry little garden.

Lots of evenings, my friends pooled together to treat me to a nice Wrexham Lager and gave me advice.

'Really, man,' they said, 'you ought to fetch her back.' They'd wipe their lips with the backs of their hands and add, 'Because we wouldn't want to see *our own wives* get any silly ideas about running off to live with this one or that, deserting us with all the youngsters to raise on our own. You're setting a poor example, Geth,' they said. They always called me Geth.

'Nooo,' I said, 'I'm doing nothing of the sort. I'm just as well without. Suits me perfectly fine.'

And that was no lie. As a matter of fact, I *was* good as ever. My eldest daughter, Edna, who'd married and had a babi of her own, nursed little Betsan, so all was well on that account. And when I looked around, I found no nagging wife to ask when I was coming home or how things were going at work or how much I'd spent at the pub or when the wood might be chopped and dried. No one asking why this and why that. None of it. A free man, I was at liberty, and yet I was surrounded by loving, obedient children. My grown and growing daughters cooked for me and cleaned for me; my sons put in the penny every week, and tiny Betsan fach, she made herself the apple of every eye at home and anywhere we went.

And didn't I have my health as well? Yes, I was a robust figure of a man with muscles on muscles, and some brains to boot. I had it all.

And when you think life couldn't get any better, it might. To top off all that, there began to be girls at the pubs. Now, first let me tell you there weren't many. Not many at all because of the dire threats ministers are always making—cuts down the numbers considerably. And they can't be seen up front in the public bar. No, they have to stay back in the secret snug through the little door in the back. You find most came from out of town and beyond the county—from cities where there were too many of them already. No local girl would even step foot in the pub—not even in a hidden snug—where someone might gawp at her, not even if she might want to. And if she did, well now, her father would drag her home by the hair or worse. Some of these out-of-town pub girls painted their lips and eyelids red and purple. You never saw anything like it years ago, but times change. And their fathers were far, far away. Their mothers, too. The days of Jenkins were well over and done with. There were many men missing—gone to war—some coming back and some never to return. I was glad enough to be too old for most of it. And even when they raised the age, I wasn't called.

Well, once the pub girls heard how callous it was when my wife upped and left me, they paid me special attention. For won't women always step in to prove they can do what another woman's left undone? Indeed, they will. There's no creature that loves a contest more than a woman. All this attention I was getting gave the workers from the south, who also relaxed at the pub, fits of envy—pure fits. Destroyed their relaxation, popped their big heads like bubbles.

None of *them* ever liked me anyway, so what did I care about it? George Morgan—him, the high and mighty—for years he'd been always painting me in ugly colours. Ever since my promotion to sub-steward. George Morgan, that yipping terrier with his yellow teeth and his white collars, with his neat fingernails coming off of his soft hands. He was always looking down his long nose on me like I was some dusty beast. Like it was just a matter of time before I'd be back cutting stone in the pissing rain instead of dry and warm beside the stove in the office as gang steward, marking my number sheets with a smile of contentment on my face. But over time, me and Morgan, we developed an understanding, I reckon. For me to tell you the details would injure Morgan and the entire Morgan family, so I'll leave it at that. I'm not the sort of man to tell tales out of school. No sir. Never was. But suffice it to say, Betsan came out of his house.

Now, the girls I was talking about, the ones at the pubs, were like barnacles, and they'd like to clamp onto a man and never let go if he had two coins to rub together. Until he didn't. For the price of a glass, they'd keep you company all night, and maybe even go out for a cart ride to boot. I wasn't a wealthy man, but my boys were all bringing in pay, some in the mines, some in the quarry—I could keep a young woman on my arm any night I chose, if I chose. And I did. And whatever some might think, there's no shame in it for me. A healthy man has needs. And I'm a healthy man with needs *and* principles. No shame in that. I'll say it again: N-O shame in that. If Aderwen was up that hill picking beans and knitting with Aggie Monroe, I was down in town having myself a time. It was her left me no choice.

To and from the pub I drove in my lovely mule cart—and it was a fine piece of craftsmanship. Hewed and built strong back in '16. I may have been a stone worker at heart and steward by smarts, but I made a fine cart as well as if it was in my very nature. My cart was the envy of many, for all men have use of a cart and mule in some way.

When I retired on my good quarry pension, some days I drove little Betsan to the school house. She stowed her blue wool school bag under the bench while we rolled along the high road. If the weather was nice, she walked, but if it was stormy or cold at all, I always gave her a lift there. I was her brilliant dada, she said, and she'd no mama at all.

That brought a tear to my eye, and I said to her 'well, babi bach, all I can say is a midwife handed you to me on the road, and I couldn't bear to put you in the orphanage, you a lovely little thing,' I told her.

She'd smile and pat my cheek, 'Well, good Dada, I don't much like the look of that orphanage up the hill. Ugly, it is.'

Truth be told, I was never such a father to the older children, but my old age opened my heart to this one and I cared for her tenderly like an old nain would. Proved my goodness upon her, I believe. I'm a good man. And I don't know of many others who'd take a foundling onto himself with no wife caring for it. No, can't say I do. It's true to say that my own father hardly glanced at me his whole life long, and when he did, was to spot my location so he would throw a punch at me without missing.

But then again, I wasn't a girl, was I?

The darkest day of my life was the day I came to fetch Betsan fach from Nefin school and she wasn't there. I'd parked the cart along the road; I'd brought her red shawl and little blue mittens from home in my pocket, as the sky was clouding. I knew she'd be glad for them in the mist, was thinking I should've reminded her to take them in the morning, and her poor little hands must have been cramped cold on the way to school, but I'd been flat with such a headache from a bad pint or two the night before that I hadn't woken to hear her leave.

Other children funnelled out of the school like winter mice, heads down to the cold wind, but no Betsan. Maybe, I reckoned, she was kept behind by the teacher for drawing on her desk again. I waited. I waited some more, as you do when a child's late, head throbbing yet from the night before. I had a nip from my flask to cure it, which I keep for rare occasions only, strapped to my leg.

Still no Betsan, so in I went. Searched everywhere—behind slate-board, under desks, in the toilet outside—but no luck. Teacher saw me and said my babi bach was not in school all day. Thought she was home ill. No, no, I was certain she wasn't at home. Wasn't a big enough house to miss a soul, no matter how little she might be. I drove home as fast as I could anyway, to be sure. I tossed blankets from beds, flung open wardrobes. No Betsan.

Might have fallen down the well! Looked in. Too dark. Couldn't see. Shouted down, 'Betsan! Betsan!' Only my echo came up.

But she might be *drowned!* is what I thought. So, I lowered the pail and listened for the sound of it hitting a body. Again and again. It seemed like only water, but how could I tell? And what if she was under the water deep where the pail couldn't reach?

Police and neighbours organised an official search, asked all the children if they'd seen Betsan that morning, but none had. Or else they couldn't be sure. Coppers made a lot of noise banging lanterns and long pikes as they looked down the well. So much noise! I thought my skull would split and jump off my neck. No Betsan. They barged into every cottage and barn, marched up and down roadsides, spread out along the strand. Leave it to coppers to make noise and find nothing. No Betsan. They talked idiocy:

'Maybe the little girl is hiding; she's sure to come home sooner or later.'

'Hiding?' I said. '*Hiding? Hiding?* No child of mine hides!'

'No need to get aggressive with us, Geth,' they said. 'We've done our best.'

I looked at them doing their best. Poking around finding nothing at all. It's then that I knew some evil man must have done something to my babi bach. I was sure. Maybe a *gipsy*. They're notorious for spiriting away the children. Or worse, maybe a bad one from the next town over. Or more likely, a neighbour. Yes, a neighbour.

But which *one*?

I raged in and out of doors. I threatened men on the road—those I knew and those I'd never seen face of before as they'd come in with the coppers. Constable said I'd better stop or else be sent to hospital, and not for any short time either. Said he understood my worry, but shouting and pushing wouldn't help a bit. I agreed to stop threatening passers-by. Instead, I went back into the pubs and drowned my sorrows there as there was no more I could do. It was easy enough—every man stood in line to treat me to a drink, having heard the news. I drank glass after glass till I collapsed.

After a while, the search was called off. They all gave up. But I didn't stop. I scoured each ravine and peered over the edge of each cliff, searching and calling. For months. Years. The rest of my life, truth be told. No telling what can have happened to a babi bach gone missing—none of it good. None of it.

That was 1924 when she upped and vanished, and in '42 I was still looking, looking for the dear skeleton by this time. Mind you, it's not that I was searching all day long. More that wherever I went, I kept my eyes open for her. Kept my head down.

That's how the rest of my life went: searching by day and sometimes by night, after the pub. I slept at odd times and was fed by my big old woman daughters. And mainly tolerated by their husbands who were always a bit resentful, if you ask me.

I'd once heard from the postman who had a regular stool in the pub that the bones will wash ashore years after a death. He said he read all about it in a mystery magazine he was delivering, that frequently he read other people's magazines as he walked, and he'd developed the skill of reading and walking as well as a Chinese scholar, he said.

'No harm done,' he said, 'and they never know.'

I told him to hurry up and tell me about the bones. I wasn't so interested in his reading practices. Then he leaned in close to tell me more about bones—everything he knew. It wasn't a lot, but it gave me something to chew on. After that, I made it my habit to drive my mule right onto the strand to look.

On the night I died, I'd been well-fortified at the public house—heard stories told and the odd song sung well. I'd gone all the way out to Pwllheli for some fresh faces. I left there after midnight, with the moon full and the tide low. The war had taken over everything. It was all anyone talked about anymore. All anyone thought about. Except for me. All I thought about was Betsan. That night, I found myself on the one smooth part of the strand, almost alone. No one ever paid any mind to what an old man and cart were about, and I was left in peace as I picked up shells and bits of wood. I held them to the moonlight to make sure they weren't bones.

The winkle picker gave me a wide berth, as they always do, his nose down in his work. I was packing things up, tightening my flask and setting some of the better shells I'd found in the cart for the rock and shell garden I'd begun keeping at the house, when the very war itself broke out above me. The planes must have been rumbling toward the coast and toward me for some time, but in those last days I was always lost in a foggy head and searching. When I did hear them, they were directly overhead, and the winkle picker was busy saving himself, scrambling up the stony cliff like a marten after rabbit, but I was old and slow—and there's nowhere to hide on the strand. The bloody Krauts were right above, firing and taking fire from what looked like the glorious RAF, though who can be sure when things happen so fast and it's so dark. There were two of those planes, and the big one dropped its bombs into the sea, and then down, fast, slicing the air. I watched, rooted to the shingle. But then came the German bomber itself, and directly under it was my cart, my mule, my shells, my flask, and my self.

I could not get out of its way.

And so, here on the beach I am yet, watching what piles up on the shore at low tide. Sometimes I see bones now, but I've got no way to tell if they're hers.

The Significance of Stones in a Man's Life

Huw Priddy • 1872-1943

I worked hard, and I'm glad of the rest now. I shifted stones, shifted stones, shifted stones my whole life. It was always me you'd see following behind farmers' ploughs with my eye to the earth, spotting what needed to be lifted and lugged away. They come up from under after the plough passes, and no matter how many ages a field's been worked, there's always more stones to come. A man can never truly see what's going on down there under the soil, not without digging or blasting, but a son of the soil like me, who's been dealing with stones his whole life, will sense shifts underfoot, no digging nor blasting needed. People think stones are heavier than earth so they must be sinking, but it's not so. Stones are coming up.

Mind you, there's rocks as well as stones, and they are not the same thing at all. Many a man has called me the rock mover, but that's not right. That could never be right. Listen here now, stones are only parts of rocks. Rocks are the big thing that gets broken into stones—or blasted or chiselled or smashed if you're talking about quarries and mines. Now, sure enough, nature does some blasting and chiselling and smashing of her own, but she's too slow for a person to see. Nature's got her own pace, and you don't have long enough to see much of it besides the seasons, which are her fastest thing. What's more, when nature does the job, it won't look like what men would make. No, not like men do it at all. When nature makes herself stones, they come in all shapes and sizes and none just like the other, even from the same rock. It's like snowflakes or fingerprints. If that happened at the quarry over up, the steward would drop his pipe, shout his head off and sack the entire crew. That's the difference between the way men will control a thing and the way nature will let it come. Nature likes difference and men want sameness.

Now, when you spot the pointy bit coming up through a field, well, that's only a hint. Yes, there's the pointy bit poking up there, looking you in the eye, and it might be that's more or less all there is, just the point with nothing much below. But maybe you've got the mountain's mother right there under you. And she'll never budge. Now, if that's the case, if you've got the mountain's mother below, what ever are you to do?

Well, I'll tell you what you're *not* to do. You've got to clear that field for planting, no matter what, so are *not* to give up. Instead, you might scalp away the top of the rock with chisels and hammers—hard work that, and a week's worth, lying on the earth and chiselling away—till you've got to a workable depth so the rock won't menace the farmer no longer. And when you've done that— and believe you me, it's a job you'll never forget—then you cart over loads of soil to cover it back to a ploughing depth, soil to hold a lifetime. It'll break your back. Where you get that soil, well, that's another problem to solve. In the end, though, your farmer will be grinning ear to foot. But that rock's coming back up sooner or later, maybe for the farmer's son or his grandson, and won't they be surprised? But I always reckoned a man can only look out for so many years' worth of strife, be he a farmer or a stone shifter.

Rocks and stones alike are the main breakers of plough shares; in some ways stones being even worse because they like to get dragged along spinning like a top. A broken share is ruination, and farmers are generally looking to avoid ruination, which they rightfully feel is always coming their way from the soil below or the sky overhead.

Far as I know, me and my dat before me were the only professional stone shifters in these parts. Some might think it's a waste and why can't a fat farmer do it for himself, but the thing is, a farmer that stops ploughing or planting or harvesting is a farmer losing money hand over fist, because he's losing time, so if he's equipped to pay at all, he's better off to have me in.

Now, if you look up and down this country lane here, and if you see through the fog where it likes to hang low by that line of scrubby trees dipping in with birch in the middle, there's walls of stone from what's been pulled, heaved, and hauled, one at a time over centuries. And all the top layers carried by me or my father before me. Him of the same name as mine: Huw Priddy. Before us, farmers had to just grub out and do it themselves.

Now the old man, he once worked at the quarry in the clanging and blasting, but he didn't get on with the new steward who was the son of the old steward, and it wasn't long before he got the sack. The young one, he always said, had been making an example of him. Now my dat, he knew nothing *but* stones and rocks already, from working as a quarryman. And you can't start a quarry all on your own. He was without a plan. And so there he was, storming home after his sacking, worried almost to death about what it would be like watching his little ones starve away. About telling my mam that was the end and maybe he'd have to ship out somewhere to try to earn a living and send it back, for he was sure the new steward would blacklist him up and down the county. Dat didn't have a holding large enough to keep them fed without the pay, not near. And it was a let as well, so there was rent to pay. He was wondering, too, should he lurk behind a tree waiting for the steward, leap out upon him and throttle him dead? At least he'd have some satisfaction in that case. And it wouldn't make matters that much worse for him. He was still a young man then, with energy for leaping out and throttling. But he couldn't be sure of the right choice so he just mumbled to himself and kept walking. That's how he told it to me, anyway.

So, there he was storming homeward, his empty pipe clamped down between his grim lips like to break it, when who should he spot but the Farmer Brynmor Evans throwing a pure fit out in his hayfield. The man was kicking at a stone he couldn't get out, and with his bare foot too, which must have hurt like fire. A man who kicks stones has lost control of himself top to bottom and probably should give himself a talking to. But this Evans was prone to it. If you think every farmer's a gentle soul, you've not known farmers. Only some are. Farming is a hard life and apt to breed the gentleness out of many a man. The sun was threatening to set on Evans with his field not ploughed and his toes swollen black and blue. My father said the man looked like the very diafol himself out there in his screeching tantrum. And there's nothing like seeing the foolishness of another man's temper to calm your own temper down.

Now, my dat, he was a helpful sort of man in general, so he put his pipe in his pocket and went over to push Evans aside, neighbourly as he suddenly felt himself to be. And he got to wrenching that big grey stone out. It was keeping him from having to go home, you see. He shouts to Evans, 'Alright now, why don't you just sit down there and catch your breath? I'll have this out for you, for I'm a man knows stone, and I've got nothing else doing on this fine day as those bastards up over just sent me packing.' Evans agreed they were bastards up over and told him he'd be grateful beyond measure if Dat could oust that stone. And he did. He got that stone loose and up. Took him till nightfall, but would have taken Evans at least two days, and Evans knew it, he did. He said to my sweating father he'd have more work for him presently. And there'd be payment in it.

That first stone was a proper one, and in the end they'd had to hook Evan's old mule to a sledge for dragging it away as no man could carry it or roll such a monster. There're certainly times that it takes a beast's help in the end. That's why I've always got my old cob alongside me in the field. He's happy enough to just chew grass and watch bumbles, but when he's needed he's on the job alright. You can't beat a Welsh cob for work and honest work at that.

Now, Evans paid my father in gammon that first day, with the agreement that Dat would come back the next day and the day after that, at no extra charge, for the gammon was large and too precious for just one day's labour. And so, my father stayed with Farmer Evans until the whole field was ready to plant, and he moved every stone bigger than a crab apple. Back at home, we all smacked our greasy lips over salty gammon.

So, you could say, my father was the one who came up with the idea of shifting stones as a business. But you can't credit him with coming up with the whole idea of shifting stones, though. No, people have been shifting these stones up north here since the cold, wet, wild dawn of time. Since they were apes, apes entirely. Which is another interest of mine—apes and long-ago creatures, but I'm getting to that.

Stone shifting's the kind of work lets a man enjoy some time for thinking about troubles and wonders alike, as it's slow going and doesn't take heavy thought to itself. Farmers got their own work to do and they're not leaning in to watch every move while you pull the stones up. You might light your pipe at the edge of the tree-line and have a good smoke as you like, and while you do that, you might get to thinking about something like *evolution*.

So, there I was—can you vision me?—in all different fields, cap pulled down against sun or rain or wind, knees on the hard earth, midwifing the stones from the ground, grunting and groaning, but all the while thinking whatever I liked in my own head. No one could stop me. I thought back over all the men and women, the ancient ones who'd come to life on this patch. I thought about how they looked back before they were human. When they were still full of fur and wildness.

At night, every night, when my Carwen was alive and well, after she finished rubbing my aching muscles with duck fat and salt, I'd put a nice dry plug in my pipe, sit pulling on it and think some more. Like any man, I enjoyed a good stare into the fire, the heat of it drying out the cold and wet of the day, baking away the rheumatism and dampness. When my boy Cadog was old enough to lend a hand, he'd come out to the fields and pick up the smaller stones while I taught him the ropes. And at the end of those days he'd sit beside me warming himself by the fire, wishing he had a pipe of his own, and me wishing I could give him one. I always knew in his heart of hearts he was sweet on that fancy girl Lili Morgan. I'm sure he thought it was a secret, but I was young once, and there's no mistaking when a boy's gaze lingers the way Cadog's did on that Morgan girl. Unmistakable. My Carwen would have said Lili Morgan and her type were not for Cadog, that Cadog needed to set his sights on someone stable and solid. She wouldn't have been wrong. But she wouldn't have been right either. Either way, she was gone, and I had other sons to help me later if Cadog was swept away on the arm of the lovely Lili to far off lands. In fact, I was hoping for Cadog to win over that Morgan girl. I am the type to always cheer for the underdog, and more than that, my

Cadog was every bit good enough for the likes of Lili Morgan or any girl out there. He was. But it wasn't to be.

Still, we did get to sit steaming ourselves dry by the fire and staring in, as men and boys do. So many days were heavy wet with mist or pure rain, and always the wind liked blowing down on us so cold we could have left the fire blazing and never been too warm, even on spring or autumn nights. There was summer, but it was short to me. Autumn, winter, spring made up most of the year. And there was cold and wet to be had in each, though that's not me complaining. I handle the weather like a ram does along the cliff. But no one can say it doesn't tend to cold here. When my wife Carwen was with me, we often found ourselves sparking the flint even in summertime, as neither of us cared for damp in the house. Snug as bugs, us there in our little cottage with the landlord knocking when he liked and a small savings box up high on the mantle. With the savings box we had, we weren't rich, but we could stay calm even in wintertime when stone shifting slowed right down to nothing. We knew we'd be back in it as soon as spring cracked.

All winter, reeking of duck fat and drawing down on the lovely tobacco—though never wasting it for it was dear—that's when I could think most deeply about the human apes I learned we are. It doesn't take much mind work to see clearly how some of your neighbours are still a bit more apish than others. And then to imagine Evans and Gethin and some of the rest coming down from the trees, all long arms and funny walks. Something so easy to imagine feels more like a memory than a heretical idea. Now, I don't know what made the apes or the earth or the sun or the rocks or none of that, but I *do know* I cannot for the life of me get my mind behind Adam and Eve. That tale just won't work when you get to adding and subtracting children and grandchildren, generations and such. And the same goes for Noah and his ark. Anyone can see the job at hand collecting every beast and living thing. Even here, in *Sir Gaernarfon*—as they once called this part of Wales—in this part alone, there's loads of creatures and too many for any one family to herd up—two of each—and then drive, carry, and drag the protesting animals onto some ark he's also building; even with the help of sons, I can't credit it. And *Sir Gaernarfon* is small compared to Wales itself, and Wales is tiny compared to the rest of the world. Oh, it's a story for children and for men made childish.

I don't mean to hold forth on it, but I've put my eye up to photos of all sorts of creatures in the magazines down at my friend Jones's place, and some so large! Take elephants for instance. If you crammed two of them on a ship, there'd hardly be room for nothing else at all, and then you'd have the hippos to deal with, and the rhinos, too. And then giraffes, deer and antelope of every stripe. Bears galore! You see what I'm getting at. And then, if you managed to fill up a ship with beasts, there's nothing for it but they will soon be hungry and one eating the next, or eating you. A lion and a piglet? A hawk and a mouse? On one boat? No.

And I'm only thinking of the creatures I know of, now. Imagine how many there are no man has even seen yet, all the growling and flying things deep down in jungles and on islands remote and far flung. Not to mention all the tiny flying and creeping things, and the things so small we can't even see them at all, but they are alive, mind you, as alive as any other thing living. I've got a magnifying glass I keep in my side pocket, and I'll tell you, there's a lot that's tiny, a lot a man can see with a little help of that sort, which he could never see without. All what's squirming or slithering or rambling along peacefully in the dirt, minding its own business.

On top of that—and this beats all the rest—I know from my own eyes, magnifying glass or no—there are some creatures that once were but are no longer. They're there as fossils, pressed right into rocks and stones, and look as you might, you won't find a living thing like them in the sea these days, nor on land.

What they say is, Noah, he did what he was told and got to live; everyone else, the great many wicked, they got to drown, every last soul shouting and gasping in the water, women and children as well, had to be babis too, all while that proud Noah floated away, holier than thou. That's the threat of the story, you see, do what you're told or drown, and if there's one thing I don't like, it's a threat.

And what does obedience get a person, anyway? In the end, it gets a person nothing, I say. Take my Carwen for instance. She was obedient to God, so obedient that she sat up at night waiting for the fickle cachwr to come and have a cup with her, and he never did. Oh, she told me a fib or two to cover for him, but I know how he left her waiting, stood her up proper, and her suffering as she did at the end, cancerous lumps come to murder her. Oh, how she hoped he'd come to save her, but never did he.

Poke your head around out into the world, will you? There you'll see many a heartless *chopsy clebran** strolling down country lanes like these, market baskets in hand, spreading gossip, committing all manner of unkindnesses, and they'll be women free of lumps, lump-free and full of life, living it up to old age and beyond. And then my Carwen, taken young, though there was no woman to match her for goodness.

And to top it off, here's me, crusty stone-grubber, refusing to set foot in capel from the day my Carwen died. Crusty me without a single obedient, godly bone in my body and still, I lived excess years. Excess years and more. Plenty of time to get tired of life and ready to go. And then, even when I did die, I had the pleasure of dropping while hard at work, never an idle day but an old man

---

*   A mouthy/argumentative chatterbox

altogether. A split second of pain and then, here I am, just waiting in the field still.

When it comes down to it, we're expected to yoke up to this god, but we can't tell if he's a cachwr with blackest sense of humour, or else just couldn't be bothered. Who can tell? I know this, though. He never saved my wife. Nor my boy, neither. Nor people ever, really. No, friend, I'm not having *him*. And before you go blaming the devil, don't bother. No, I've thought that one through and you can't blame The Bad Man and say it's The Big Man in charge all at the same time, not when it's one that fashioned the other in the first place. It's all a ball of hot wax.

And if you think a man can just walk away from it all peaceful, think again. Ministers are forever jumping out from around corners in black, like ghouls—startling the *Iesu* out of a person—always after a coin or two in the plate, going on and on in my face like it would coax me back in line for the sake of the young ones. It never would.

My ways of thinking weren't welcome with many, but that's partly why I was happy to have my friend Gwil Jones down at his shop. Now there was a man who understood what I was up against. Jones was a fellow glad to light my pipe with his silver lighter. Glad to tell me what I was: 'You're agnostic, friend, and be content with it, would you?'

'Now, what's that word mean?' I asked.

'That means *undecided*,' Jones says, '*undecided*, and *that* means you're not for the god team nor for the devil team, not for the Mohhamedans or the Hindus either. No, agnostic means you realise there's no one knows for sure what's what when it comes to the biggest wonders. And not all wonders are magnificent. Some are only sad.'

I think about that, and it sounds about right.

'Takes an honest man to be agnostic,' he says, looking me directly in the eye. 'Now take me, for instance. I'm an atheist these days. That means I'm done with any god entirely, I'm sure there's no such thing and I'm not afraid to say it to you'

You have got to give it to Jones. He's thought it all through. He looks into things all the way to the bottom. And it matters to him what he calls himself. Me, I'm not sure if I am agnostic, to tell the truth, because I'm not even trying to decide what I am anymore. Either way, I just don't care. Because all the caring in the world doesn't change what is or is not.

Though, now, honest to you I say, if any god showed up in my face, right here in this field, I'll tell that great *nothing* I'm finished with him anyway. I'd also say he's taken his time coming. But it's as likely that he'll show up as that I'll spy *Ysbaddaden** stomping like the giant he is over the mountain, crushing townspeople left and right under his massive feet. And of the two, God and *Ysbaddaden*, I'd much rather chew the fat with the old giant. I'd light his pipe for him, I would. Me and him and Jones, we'd have a grand old time.

But no giants or gods ever came, and so it was just me and Jones every Sunday because neither one of us belonged in capel anymore. One particular Sunday when all the others were praying away, I remember it was spring for the way the sleet was trying to come in under Jones's shop door. Jones and I were there, discussing the way Gethin met his end under that plane. Wasn't gossip, really. Just an astounding and satisfying little tale. If you knew Twm Geth, like us, you'd not have felt bad about it at all. One thing I always liked about Jones: he could talk about things in an interesting way and stay just this side of gossip. His fireside there at the shop was a warm spot, and I always liked the piles of stuff Jones keeps there. He kept all sorts of books and magazines and

---

*   Mythical giant of Gwynedd

curiosities, also spoons, and fabrics and strange dolls, so much stuff in a sort of neat jumble. I'd never know what he might bring forth to show me on any Sunday, or to read aloud to me.

Now, on this particular one, he pulls out the big Bible there, a fat one, which is written in Welsh and then an even fatter one written in English, with extra illustrations. He says he got them half price when a religious school moved places. He tells me, 'Friend, I'm going to read you the parts they never give out in any church or capel or cathedral known to man; sit back, friend.'

He almost smiles all the while, reading lists of countless punishments, warnings, happenings. He's flipping the pages with great relish, thin and dry as they are, Gwil Jones is. And he saves the best for later, like any good story teller. He makes his way to daughters in the family way by their fathers, then people turned to stone and entire families wiped out just to test a man's loyalty. Now, I'd heard these before in capel, but you know, the telling makes all the difference. As does the company. You hear it clear at Jones's shop.

Soon Jones is slapping his own knee like he's riding a fast horse in the races and winning. Both of us laughing, and it's not even the whisky's got us doing it. It's comfort, I think. And not having to worry about what someone else thinks. It's ease.

'Maybe the preacher down the road should read a bit of this part or that from the pulpit on Sunday morning,' he says. 'give the good parishioners something salty to really chew on!'

He adds that good study of Leviticus might put the barbers out of business with all the rules against shaves and haircuts, and he'd like to see that. He'd like to see mothers stopped from giving out kitchen table haircuts up and down the county. Just to see it. All the men and boys weighted down by long hair, like Irish pirates from times gone by. He says he used to be a more serious man once, but that's left him entirely these days. He says, friend, you got to choose to laugh or not to. I'm choosing to. He wipes his hands together as if he's got a delicious supper in front of him.

By the time he gets to the very best of the Bible, a peculiar rule about how a woman's hand should be chopped off if she were to grab her husband's fighting opponent by his bollocks, the tears are wetting the old floor and there's us rolling and howling.

The door is locked up and there's no customers to see or hear. I'm shouting 'show her no mercy!' as it says in the Bible, 'you must! You must!' And there's Jones, as if he's an actor on a grand stage, one hand protecting his tender bollocks from armies of grabby biblical women. He turns his back to the crowd that's not there and waves his one free arm, desperate, 'no ladies, please, Deuteronomy says you *mustn't!*' And that's his last word before he falls to the floor with a thump, a grand ending to our little play. He lays there a minute or two just gazing up at his ceiling and then brushes off his jumper and climbs back into his chair.

'So,' says Jones, once we've recovered, 'I'm a bloody atheist and you are a stinking agnostic, for now, and just about everyone who lives around us is all for believing this particular collection of tales and rules. Many would say we are *heretics*, friend,' he says, 'and that's the condition, Huw bach, that we are in, and where's the surprise?'

None, I say, none with both of us mourning a wife and a son, apiece, none at all. And him all those babis he never talks about. You mix a thinking man with grief, and this is what you get, stories soon fall away.

Jones poured us a clear yellow drink from a tall bottle, something from the continent he kept locked up tight with keys under the register, and we drank it from blue and white china cups he took down from the sales shelves, us toasting each other again and again. It's no small thing to have a friend in this world who thinks mainly like you do.

But it wasn't the only time we did so; no, most Sundays whilst the good people of town were praying away in capel we had such talks. Gwil Jones and me, content there, sampling the best spirits Gwil had to offer, and entertaining ourselves with lively Bible stories, magazine articles, books of history, what have you—it was a regular variety show, Jones always said.

His housekeeper sometimes came rushing in with a tray of scones, letting the bells over the door ring loudly as she hurried back out on her way to capel herself. Prone to slamming doors, she was. She loved capel, did the lovely Yolanda, but capel did not love her. She loved it even though the air always went dead by the time she reached the narthex, sucked silent by the other parishioners, who were sure beyond certain that she was a fallen woman; it was only Christian charity, the watchful eye of the minister, and some element of the law stopped some of those women stoning our Yolanda, which Leviticus clearly calls for if you listen carefully. We have plenty of stones around here for the job, but there was no question in the end—they would let her live for their own satisfaction. Something to talk about. I once told her she'd better hope the congregation never took to reading that book on their own, and wouldn't she rather stay back at the shop with us and have some good conversation? Yolanda glared and slammed the door on her way out, taking with her the pies she'd brought for us. She never was much for the subtle sense of humour, and that was a shame all around.

That day of the yellow drink, I thought about how Yolanda is like Pascal; she figures she might as well go to capel just in case, just in case it's all true. That's called the divine wager, you know, but I don't see much divine about it, more like working to save your arse on the outside bet.

If they have a lake of fire to cast me into, so be it, let the pitching begin. But I'll have my answers, by god I will! Jones says apes are luckier than us, that we evolved too far for our own good.

But then he lights our pipes and takes it back because apes can't read, apes can't enjoy the finer things, which Jones can and does. I don't put much store by fine things, not to say I don't enjoy them when they come my way, but I think it might be worth losing it all to be wise like apes again. I say so, and Jones just laughs and pours us another. But I know he's not laughing at me. So, it's alright.

Once Yolanda asked me this when she was dropping scones by the shop, she asked me, if I found out that there was a God—'because there *is*,' she said—and he had taken my wife and my boy into heaven and they were happy up there, playing harps all day and singing and dressing in gowns of ivory silk or something close enough to it, then would I forgive God?

I told her I'd think about it.

But Jones, he closed his eyes and said, 'for God's sake, Yolanda, playing harp all day, every day, that's all there is to do there? If that's the case, it's a good thing I'm atheist or else I'd be eaten alive with anger if I was to get roped up with God and his perpetual play-school! Playing harp for eternity, *achan*!"* He laughed and laughed, which was out of character for him in his dealings with Yolanda—he was almost always stiff as a statue with her. That time the scones hit the floor before she left.

I always did my best not to gawk at the photo of Jones's wife and boy that he perched up near the register. But I couldn't help it. Really, I could never help but look at things that made me curious, but especially them two. Likely because I never had a photo of Carwen nor my own boy who died, poor, lovely Cadog. Nor of

---

*   Man as an endearment or emphasis. Like the American use of 'what's up, man'

the family altogether. Never had it done. I suppose I thought I had time later. Besides, back then it was very dear and we weren't made of money. Jones has more than his share in that regard.

So, there I was, always stealing side glances at Jones's dead wife and child to remember what a wife and a boy look like before tragedy comes rolling over. Though I'd say his boy looked a bit stranger than mine did, I'm sure of it. Something wasn't right with the boy. And the wife, she had a far-away look my Carwen never had. No, my Carwen was always right there with a person. Not shy in the least. I missed her like hell.

In the end, we got old, Jones and me, older than just about anyone else we knew. But after Leviticus and before his death, we struck up a deal to do with fossils. Now, no one else knew about it because it was none of their business, no need for various noses poking around, nor for farmers wanting a cut in. But I don't mind letting the cat out of the bag now. Poor Gwil bach got a bad leg—rheumatism—and he was too old to do any travelling to collect things anymore, but that man had a drive in him, a drive to find things and sell some of them.

He wanted fossils, lots of fossils. And he said I was the man to get them. You'd have no trouble finding them if you knew what you were looking for. They are all about this place, in the *carboniferous limestone,* millions and millions of them. In his shop, Jones has lots of books, and when he first asked me to hunt fossils, he showed me the photos and taught me the proper names for them. He said he knew I wanted to know what they really were, and he was right. I wanted the Latin names. I wanted all the Latin names in my mouth because that's the height of knowing anything, that and the history of the creature. So, I memorised them.

At first, I swear, I couldn't see fossils in any stones or rocks. It seemed that they must all be in the south, and I feared Jones had made a mistake, sending me on a fool's errand. After all, that famous rock hunter Salter found all of his in the south. But Jones said, 'No, no, Wales is small, man—if you ever go travelling you'll see so—and if they're in the South, they're surely in the North as well. Keep looking while you're pulling up rocks,' he said.

'Stones,' I said, 'no one pulls up a rock.'

'Man,' he said, 'you're finding your feet and I stand corrected. Just put your eye on the stones.'

And he was right. Slowly, slowly, my eyes got sharper, and after a year or so squinting at stones and rocks in my new way, putting my face up close until the farmers were sure I'd gone out of my mind or I needed spectacles, I began to spot fossils everywhere, And once I could see fossils, there was no time for deep wonderings about gods and devils and dead wives and sons hardly at all. It was the main thing on my mind. Every stone might hold a secret creature. It was the most exciting prospect every day and all day as I dug. And then at home, even alone with my pipe and the quiet fire, even rubbing the duck fat on my aching muscles with my own old hand, I was playing over in my mind the bits I'd found just recently and what I hoped to see next time. At night I dreamed of the fossil creatures swimming by, in colours.

Out in the fields of other men, when I lugged stones back to the piles, I'd take my thumb and peel up the mossy side to see what was underneath, and it turned out it was easier to see fossils on damp stone.

But I did it quick, because me and Jones agreed to keep quiet about our 'method of procurement,' as he called it. We didn't need a mob of fossil-hunting farmers coming out of the woodwork, which would have been the ruin of both my livelihoods.

A man doesn't gather stones, he lugs them only as far as they must go, and farmers would have thought me strange to be lugging stones away from their fields, so I waited till they went in for their meal. I ate my packed egg and cheese, piling the stones I'd take, or chipping smaller bits from big ones too much to take away. I put my fossil stones in a special pile marked with a stick in the middle, coming up like a unicorn's horn, so I could find them when I came back in the night with cob and wagon.

Gwil Jones sold my fossils in his shop, mostly to out-of-town-ers who came in the summer from down south on a jaunt—*Saeson plagus*—the annoying English—but, once in a while, to a local who wanted to have one on the cottage mantel. And Jones, he gave me thirty percent on each, thirty percent, which made us partners as much as friends.

Odd pair to be sure, but never a falling out between us. And money or no money, we loved the fossils, just touching them and knowing it was touching time before time. We kept the best ones back in the storeroom in a crate with straw, and each new haul, we spent hours looking at what I'd brought in, looking up close with the magnifying glass. Then we wrapped each piece worth keeping in white tissue paper with a little note that said type and location. I wrapped and Jones wrote, but our locations were false on pur-pose—we had a code. Never did a location look like it had come from a farm.

I kept a few fossils for myself, too. Long ago, I'd have thought of them, if I could even see them, as curly creatures or blobbed things, but now I knew what they were. They were, to my mind, like photographs of truth—no messing about with words—hard rock. I suppose hard rock truth, like that, was what I craved all the late years of my life.

I had a few small fossil stones in my jacket pocket for Jones the day he went down dead at the doorway to his shop, me just on the other side of the door trying to get in, trying to help.

You don't get a friend like Gwil Jones more than once in a lifetime. You don't.

When he was gone, I kept collecting anyway, though there was no money in it for me with him dead. I went on thinking about all of our conversations just the same as well. I thought of what he'd say about this or that, not because I didn't have thoughts of my own, but because it takes two to discuss a thing, and you learn to make do with what you have. My children all grown and out of the house, except for poor Cadog, of course, I made do. I wasn't miserable, though. Not at all. I had a warm stove, a full pipe, fossils, my own thoughts, and lots of memories stored up in me.

When I went down dead here, in Evan's north field, I was picking fossils—loading my pockets with them—some lovely crinoids or sea lilies, which aren't lilies at all but tiny little animals long gone. I planned to race down the hill, slow as I was in racing those days. I thought I'd get out of the wet, sit in front of my fire with my magnifying glass. Stick my eyeball up to fossil after fossil, figuring out the mysteries. Watch them and me dry by the fire. I had a pipe ready for me on the mantle—I'd packed it in the morning.

But I was done. Right here in the field.

Now mind you, I barely collected the tiniest cut of fossils, there's so many many more to be found, right here under you. Listen here, keep your eyes open, now. Don't just tread over them. And if you do find some, I'd like it if you left just one or two on the steps of the capel. Or else take them inside and have whoever's there explain that, would you? I'll wager you'd flummox them entirely. Capel's right down the lane on your left, back through town. I'll wait here.

The Priority One Finds Herself

Marged Dafydd • 1890-1945

Over four hundred live babis, I delivered. Most were pink and hale, taking great breaths and crying their lungs into being. But there were fifty-some still-born or nearly so, as well. Now that's including the ones I delivered alone and the ones with my gran. Yes, four hundred all told over the years. And yes, there were those who lived but sent their mothers out of this life. This can happen. Still, despite the births that end in sorrow, it's mainly a good craft, and perhaps the most important one there is. I cannot think of one that matters more.

But delivering babis isn't all a midwife does. I gave medicines to make it easier to conceive. I gave medicines to rid the womb of an unwanted one. Besides anything to do with babis, there were the old, the ancient, the crooked and tired: all mine to minister to when they came up my path. And there were medicines and prayers for every possible ailment or situation. In the old ways. And there was the other work of the midwife: death. For death and new life are the two sides of the same stone, and she who brings both forth must do so without fear. And so, I saw old souls out of this world, which is a birth as well, only in a different way.

My gran's specialty was foresight. I did not have that gift. Instead, my specialty was to remove the evil eye, and though it was my specialty, it was always the most difficult of my work, for the evil eye's cursed gaze clings tight to its intended, tighter than a caul to an infant, tighter than a skin on a worm. We are not always gifted in what comes easy to us. In all this work, I learned everything I knew from my gran, who was said to have been the finest midwife ever known in these parts. And she had learned from her gran, and that gran from her gran, and so on, back past time itself. No one can say for how many generations, but likely for all of them. And time is nothing but an imaginary red wound winding itself all around, making fools of us all; we would do best to ignore it anyway. That's what I did. I let go of time and I tended the people at their very most: *most* hurting and *most* beautiful, and I patrolled the forest, tearing off leaves of worts and lifting mats of mosses and pinching stamens most beautiful—and most tender— laying them all into my sheepskin satchel as I went. I could never help but sigh with delight at the colours and the velvety way all that looked when it came together. Pretty as a picture. If I could have painted it I would have. But we had no time for painting of that sort, or even for sighing.

My gran said it was no use to take any notice if a thing was beautiful or not, the flower, the petal, the root; the only matter, the only matter that mattered, she said, was did it work? Did it ease some ill or bring forth some benefit?

But I disagreed with her on this, and it was our main disagreement. And as we disagreed and I grew in size and age, I came to realise that she held my love of beauty against me—a fickle pride, she thought it. A sign of silliness. A flaw. I felt ashamed, but still, how could I ignore beauty spread right in front of me? I could not. And this rift was evident even as she helped me with my hair.

From the time I was a girl, Gran knotted my hair in an intricate plait-braid that protected me from the evil eye with its round loops. She said as a girl who could remove the evil eye, I must be especially protected. I was just eight when I came to live with her, and she pronounced that all my life I should wear my hair thus as it had enchantment. That it suited me. So, I have.

'It is a beautiful weave!' I said that the first time she plaited it, running my fingertips over the smooth lumps of plait, smooth like the humps of dolphins, but Gran hissed, 'No!' it's a purposeful knot and nothing but!'

'Can't it be both?' I asked.

No, was the answer. No.

And yet, the plait on my head, it was *beautiful*. No matter what anyone—even Gran—might say or not say. It could not be denied.

Gran wore her own hair in a different plait but usually with a nubby length of red cloth wrapped and tucked over it, so I saw her own knots only in the lamplight of our home, or by the hearth light, but never in the light of day. Whenever she shrugged off her bulky, old cloaks and her headscarf near the fire, she changed from a common old woman to a timeless creature. All of a sudden, her face was no longer cramped by wool and her hair shone like silver links in a curly chain. Silver it was, with some black yet underneath—like iron. Yet, her figure was straight as a pine, upright and trim. She floated over the floor; she stirred the pot gracefully; she hung the herbs from the beams like a saint blessing crowds. And she swept the floor as if dancing gently with the straw broom. Never did she conduct herself with clumsiness, with haste.

Gran had a voice for humming, and she hummed so well that you didn't wish for her to sing. And that was a good thing because she did not sing. If I asked her why, she only hummed a new tune. She was that way. She instructed me carefully in craft, but she never chatted with me. Her hands were deft and sure, but I cannot say they were soft or kind. No, certainly they weren't kind. She was known to pinch at the upper arm for careless mistakes. And she'd not be disappointed to hear that, for kindness was not much to her—not in the way most think of it. Kindness, she said, was a class of falseness. This is not to say she was cruel or mean, only that she was not kind. She did what was necessary and good but took care not to fight destiny. She reminded me over and over again to take the similar ways.

I was named after my Gran, which is why she chose me to apprentice above all my sisters, and the others were jealous. It's not that they'd ever spoken about wanting to be her apprentice, but more that they realised they might want to once they were passed over. They looked my way with open envy and knit eyebrows, with unhidden frowns, and they let me know that it was their opinion that this was a useless art I was learning. And that it suited me well. Even into our grown-up years, they kept this opinion. And yet, wasn't it true they all called upon me when they were in need? They certainly did, once Gran was gone, anyway. But I am kind, and so I went without once reminding them of how they'd done to me.

Gran's little house was as neat as Gran herself, with a tufted red wool carpet put carefully over the flagstone floor, and the flags laid so tightly that you couldn't get a toe into the seams. Her hearth was made of the same stone as the floor, and it was flanked with two painted cupboards. The one on the right held the first edition of the *Encyclopaedia Britannica*, which she'd been given by her grandmother—though neither of them could read—and which her grandmother had been given by a very important man at the delivery of a very important babe. As a gift of course; a midwife must never accept payment in money. It might seem the books would have been useless to Gran's grandmother who could not read a word, but she took the Encyclopaedias nevertheless. First, no gift for birthing should ever be refused, and second, she knew her own great granddaughters *would* read. She didn't like the idea of it, but she'd seen it coming in the way the grass blew in the wind. She, like Gran, had the gift of sight. That's why Gran sent the coin along with me to school up the hill from the time I came to her at eight until I was twelve. Things were changing underfoot, and Gran, though she bristled at it, was too wise to think it would stop coming.

In that cupboard there were also paints, which Gran made herself, and which were not for painting on a whim. She kept them in small pots, and those she used to brush symbols onto our walls—great swirls and birds and animals and stars to keep us safe from harm. Symbols to greet the ghosts of our ancestors and to keep the faeries at bay. Things to set other things in motion or stop them suddenly.

The cupboard on the left held blankets of all sorts, blankets for the newly born, for the newly dead, for the badly chilled, for the lovelorn and profusely sweating. It was a lending library of blankets coming in and out of the house. Some were much, much older than Gran herself, she said. Some before the quarry. But not before the abandoned mines. For the mines have been here always. Smaller, yes, but always here.

Dried mint kept the moths out of the blankets. My favourite was soft green wool embroidered with darker green in the shapes of oak leaves and with dark brown to make plump acorns. It had a golden fringe and was nearly worn through in places but somehow made finer by the wear. This is the way of quality things made long ago. You won't find it easilythese days. We wrapped the Morgan babi in that one and I suppose it's still at Twm Geth's house somewhere, though he's been ground out.

From Gran's rafters and beams hung the expected herbs: rosemary and sage and lavender and thyme, dried leeks. And then there were less-common herbs and plants, worts and banes, lichens and mushrooms and mosses, some hanging with the rest, some hidden away or made into tinctures and salves. The air was fragrant and the red carpet warmed the room. All my sisters wanted to live in Gran's house instead of on the quarry property where Father had taken a job and moved them. It wasn't far, but it was another world altogether.

Gran had only space and time for one learner: me. And I know I was a bit of a disappointment; I knew it then. I still know it now. It was only because I often forgot the amounts in mixtures and remedies and had to be reminded over and over of ratios and techniques. I also lost my knife almost daily, even though it was tied to a leather thong and hung from my waist. There I'd be digging through the folds in my skirts while it escaped me like a fish in the reeds.

Gran remained as she was, youngish in the house with me and looking like an honest crone in the forest and on the street. She remained this way for a very long time, scores of years, until one day she saw my own hair was going silver. We were shelling peas of a fine spring afternoon in the trellis garden at the side of the house—our garden much bigger than our one room house, and we both preferring to be out in it rather than cooped up come a fine day. We'd no mirror in the house for Gran believed that those who looked into mirrors soon forgot how to manage their own faces, so I'd no idea that the hair at the front of my head had begun to grey. I was a dark-haired woman, so the threading was noticeable to Gran from across the garden table. When she popped her last pea into the bowl, she evened her eyebrows into a straight line. Then she said, in the same steady voice she used for all occasions—except the most utterly grievous—that it was time for her to put in her order with Evans the Box. She said, when a midwife's granddaughter becomes an old woman, it's a sign that it's time for the midwife to move on. I wanted to argue and tell her no, she mustn't leave me alone yet, or I'd surely make an utter mess of things. I felt like I'd somehow killed her, and I opened my mouth to say it, but she put her finger to her lips and went indoors. I shelled my remaining peas in tears, for I knew Gran always meant what she said. And what's worse, I'd seen her *canwyll corff* shimmering near the stream in the valley the night before, while I was out collecting night water for the cleaning of ears. It's light had shone greenish and clear, and its portent is never wrong. But I denied it as long as I could anyway.

Gran, however, did not hesitate. She'd soon busied herself in weaving a burying blanket of dyed yellow wool upon her wooden loom in the evenings, tapping her foot gently on the treadles. She also stopped telling me what to do in general, and instead, asked me unending questions, the loom's beam and her head moving as she did so, and the blanket coming together like where the two rivers merge. If I answered one question wrong, some inquiry about bleeding, or croup, or gout, or breech birth, or sugar, or wind, she'd say simply, 'Now, someone has died early or lived more painfully from your error; is that what you want? Is that your wish?' I felt like an errant school girl despite the grey hair on my head. She would never tell me the answer. Never give me the correct cure or treatment. Instead, she repeated the question and let me go on accidentally murdering imagined friends and neighbours until finally I hit on the proper method. Then she nodded. Maybe I should have thought to keep making mistakes on purpose to slow down her thinking she was done with me, but it never occurred. And besides, you didn't pull the wool over Gran's eyes.

---

*   Corpse candle, a mysterious light, a sign of impending death

Feeling like I'd never remember everything, I asked Gran if I might write down instructions for myself. She said I had bloody well better not, and did I not *yet* understand that these cures were secret? Special? Ancient? I nodded. I wanted to tell her that I'd keep them to myself, in their written form, but I knew better. It was not the first time we'd had this talk.

On the last night of Gran's life, she was talkative. Bringing up the name of Betsan Gethin over a supper of hot oat cakes and a *cawl** of mushroom and greens. It was springtime. The kite was calling somewhere outdoors, high in the sky. Unseeable. Gran's eyes were dark and brimming with energy. She was thinking of the day we'd carried the tiny babi girl out of the Morgan house, Lili Morgan, hands crossed over her small breasts, eyes closed, now quiet. We left Lili to her family and took that babi no one there wanted. That hardly anyone knew existed. I suppose Gran had known for some time how she might draw out what was needed to fulfil the child's destiny.

We had met Twm Gethin amid the gorse on the low path as one passes a cat. You might think there's no way to get a man to bring home his bastard child to his wife, but there is, and Gran found it. She knew the man well. She'd delivered all his other children, delivered him, too. Terrible as he was, he was her creature in a sense. When we'd watched him march to the upper path with the babi, full of his own self and some strange vitality, I'd questioned Gran's wisdom. Silently. But she had known and turned to me saying, 'we must always watch over this child, but for now this is best. It won't be forever. And this is the type of babi who will not thrive in an orphanage. No child thrives there, but this one in particular would wither and die. No, the orphanage is not her destiny. Nor is our home. Now, make no mistake, her presence in the Gethin

---

*   Soup

house will cause pain, but that pain will bring goodness as well. We will watch her to help as needed, but don't worry, Marged, indeed it is her *destiny* to live under her father's roof for some time, and then, I feel, under the roof of her mother's kin.'

'How will Gethin explain the babi,' I asked.

Gran just shrugged.

We kept a close eye, and then when she disappeared, we were the only people unworried. For Gran had seen what would be. Gran said she would have known if the child had perished. She felt the heart was still beating and the spirit still in this realm. I nodded and assured her she must be right. But I wasn't certain myself. She instructed me that if the girl were ever to return, I must welcome her. And if she were not to return, I must light a candle for her every midwinter's day to help her along. I was also to light candles for several more she thought were in need, but it was Betsan Gethin and the tanglement of her life we contemplated as we sipped our last meal of cawl together.

She'd done her dying quietly, so quietly that despite our living together in what was really a cottage made of one large room, I did not know until I awoke in the morning—me stretching and yawning my way toward the low burning hearth, and her dead, cold and perhaps smiling in a satisfied way, a bit. I suspect she'd put some valerian in my bedtime chamomile to keep me down, but I never tasted it. No one could be *that* quiet—death has a sound.

She had prepared her own body, was washed, combed, and wearing her a shroud she'd sewn with her many amulets pinned all along the hem, alternating with feathers of owls and eagles, patterned, and decorated with raspy skins of garden snakes. Her hair looked as if she'd been brushing and plaiting it for hours—like still moonlight. She'd stained her finger tips with berry juice and pushed dried lavender up under her sleeves. I'd very little left to do but help her into the ground, which I did with the aid of my sisters and mother and father, who had come by to help. Having come on foot they needed to rest before going back, and so I had them all for two nights there in the little house that had been Gran's and was now, mine. It felt unfair to them—I knew it—to my sisters. But what could I do? A house cannot be divided. And my sisters were gracious.

We buried her body exactly as she had instructed me, in the family plot just behind the house. I followed her wishes to the smallest detail; the words, the moment, the spot. There was no minister present for the minister those days was against Gran and me and our ilk altogether, even though he'd no complaint with us coming to capel as he hoped we'd change our ways. He was against signs and symbols and medicine not done by doctors so he'd not touch us nor come to our home. For three full years after, I honoured her by collecting dew to sprinkle there—dew to help her on her way back to where it is we all come from.

My family had brought me some comfort and company—more than I'd had in as long as I could remember, but they would soon leave me to begin living alone; they never asked if I wanted to come back to them. No, I was to stay on here. My sisters and I emptied the baskets Gran had left filled near the foot of her bed. We handled what was inside: blankets—yes, more blankets—and jars of mince, a magnifying glass, a book entitled *Great Fish of the Atlantic*, some issues of *National Geographic Magazine* from America. There was a pair of fine bone knitting needles, and, at the very bottom, wrapped in three shrunken tea towels, a tin-rimmed looking glass with a dents in the tin, but no crack in the glass. This was a shock considering Gran's hatred of looking at oneself in mirrors. I promptly hung it near the door so that I could see myself before I went out. So that I could become acquainted with my own face, finally. So that I could make sure I was presentable. Because she'd known I'd find it.

My gran had been such an enormous force that without her I felt diminished. Little. But in time I began to expand. Next, I thought about a child of my own. Gran had been a midwife who had borne many children of her own, and it seemed to me that having a child might be proof that a midwife knows her work, understands pain. Gran had never said I wouldn't have one. But I suspected that she had not seen children for me. And that she didn't have the heart to tell me. By the time she died, I was nearly past the age of possibility already. And what's more, children could be a hindrance.

And yet, I wanted what I wanted.

As I grew used to working without Gran at my side, I began to realise things weren't as simple as they used to be. Times were changing faster and faster, and even the people who preferred me to that fever-spreading doctor in town had specific ideas about husbands and wives and where *babis should* come from and when—ideas unlike Gran's or mine—ideas from ministers. Most of Nefin's women went about with pious expressions and spent easily observed time at capel praying about their daily lives. And their sins. Some of which involved using my services, though in those moments, the minister was far out of sight and mind, him and the doctor as well. I had services they needed and which the doctor did not provide—not just for bringing babis but for stopping them coming as well. Girls and married women alike balanced on a circus rope between principles and needs. And I had to balance along with them. There were days I wished the doctors and the ministers and the priests would all jump into the sea and drown themselves, so that we people could get on with the business of living and dying without more worry, because simple living and dying is a busy business indeed. And much of it takes a woman's touch. And let me add, there were women who should have rid themselves of their conditions but hadn't the sense to do it. Poor Lili Morgan comes to mind.

Once I'd hung that mirror on the wall near the door and started brushing my hair out of its plaits, men of all classes and types seemed to drop out of the trees and earth and skies. As if they were sent to the last fading petals of my beauty, a beauty of which I had been previously quite unaware. I needed no enchantment at all. How sad it was to greet my own loveliness and bid it farewell at almost the same moment in that looking glass by the door. Oh, how Gran would have glowered if she had been able to see me there, turning and gazing at my own self as if drowning, sometimes mesmerised there for more than a few moments, even when someone was in great need of me. My eyes were green and changing! My hair still ebony underneath, if silver on top. My skin milky and pink on most days, except on my down days when I became pallid. My brows near black and arched. There was a dimple in my right cheek when I smiled, and I smiled at myself in the mirror sometimes. It felt fine enough at that time. And I enjoyed being alive.

Of the men, I chose a handful—a good-sized handful—to have some kind of romance with. I deserved it by then. Like the different sort of herbs of forest and field, I found them to be varied, but curing and tonic, mostly. They were single men, or widowed, and looking, I suppose, for a wife.

Yes, I enjoyed them, but I never truly trusted them, for hadn't I been raised by an old woman alone, my grandfather gone by the time I'd come? I'd never seen a woman bend to a man. There was my own mother and father, of course, but I left them when young, and my mother was none too pliant, herself, going her own way as a rule. These men, though, they expected some level of bending. Took it for granted. Expected some level of me wanting their advice on a great many things. But I knew my craft and my life and had no questions for them. And I soon tired of it when more than one suggested I give up healing and take up baking in its stead.

Perhaps I'd seen far too many ghastly things done to the bodies of women to take on a man so late in life. The bruises on the wives and daughters, the babes gotten before proper time since the last, the wearing out of good women by selfish breeding; the welts on Gladys Evans, the awful death of poor Lili Morgan, her slender body nowhere near ready for what it had no choice in. And the story Gran had told me about Cranstal Jones up there, frozen in grief each time a daughter was taken by the cot death, with Jones himself somehow looking more than a little guilty. Hands up under his armpits as he held them from then on.

I thought about the ravenous hunger a woman can have, the need, the desperation. About Yolanda Monroe, the red-haired servant girl who marched up here from Shop Jones place demanding a love enchantment from Gran only to be sent away in tears. I thought about the mirror and the men it brought to me, and my stomach turned against the whole lot for once and for all. I bolted my door to them from then on. I made sure to plait my hair the way Gran taught me again, and I got on with healing the people, especially the married women; for their lives, you see, were so very hard. Harder than many will admit to.

I laboured long, travelling the roads day and night to help my neighbours, and I did it mainly quite well. And for a long time. During my last year, after a particularly nice cup of sorrel tea, I took down the mirror from the wall like Gran would have wanted, and it felt good. Some long time later I burned all the notes I'd written myself: incantations I was afraid to forget, recipes for tonics, tinctures, even those for treacle and ratios for custard and lists of people to visit. I burned them all up. They were for my use alone. Oh yes, I'd collected quite a horde of papers, against Gran's warnings, and with no little childish relish I'd been scribbling away since she'd gone. They floated up the chimney in lit ash only to drift down to the trees and settle along the near-forest floor.

Days after I'd finished, I was arranging my satchel and noticed my small silver shears were missing, probably left out by the sloe-berry again; I was always mislaying them. Rummaging in Gran's ancient rosewood box for a second pair, I happened upon a bit of paper folded into the shape of a boat, smudged with purple stains. It was with great slowness that I carefully un-tucked the ends and then pressed the paper flat against the old wooden mixing table, ironing it with the palm of my hand. I was nervous and hesitated to read the words that now showed, scant though they were, for it must be something strange. No notes lived in this house unless I'd written them, and this was not mine. In strong and yet shaky hand—which looked like the hand of the old spinster school teacher down the road who must have taken dictation from her— was written what I read aloud in a whisper.

> *Marged,*
>
> *I have some sorrow with me tonight, for I know you have felt that I have been hard on you and you do not know why. Because of this, and against my way, I have had this written down for you in hopes that you may find it when needed. You required hardness of me as the hacking catarrh requires dark honey, or as nettles can make a tonic. But also know I have loved you excessively in my way. I am as I am. I have been as I was made.*
>
> *Marged, your grandmother*

Glad to have found her words, I surely was, but I also questioned her spirit; why make me wait so long? Couldn't she have put it in the biscuit tin where I'd have surely stumbled upon it within days of her death? It would have made fine reading with a drop of tea and a shortbread biscuit or two. Then I apologised to her spirit, for Gran would have found this no joking matter, my levity offensive. We were not at all the same, she and I, despite our name.

Finally, though—and much more quickly than I ever thought it would come—it was time to prepare my own self. I ordered my own coffin from Evans. I readied my body as Gran had done hers, but with far less certainty than she had. I was never as brave as she. And even as I did this I felt sad and more than a little frightened of death. But I talked myself back to what must be. I may not have been as old as Gran had been, but I was older than many I'd eased into their graves, and I felt it coming on—in the night, the emptiness approaching would wake me. And I knew the signs of sickness that spoils the insides of a woman, the thinness despite plenty of food, the thirst without hunger, the constant sleepiness. I accepted it. As one must. For not everything can be cured and we all must die.

The people would miss me—on occasion—I mused. For we Welsh, despite changing times, always respected our wise women. And who would be there to greet Betsan Gethin should she return? Though she would be a full-grown woman by now and likely able to handle herself. Or no, maybe they would not miss me at all. So regular were doctors by that time it seemed midwives would all disappear forever. But regardless, those I healed and mended and birthed, they would remember me kindly. I felt sad that some preferred to enter and leave the world in a hospital, to which they often sped in cars and ambulances, shrieking away from the countryside and towards big buildings. Horse and cart, though rarer now, clattered toward the hospital if they could. Not I. I would remain home. I felt like it was not just me passing on but my way of life entirely—our way of life.

It was four nights before I happened upon the right night to go; I was not precise in knowing when. I was never a precise woman outside of dosing. I slowly prepared myself a draught of a special mix of powerful plants and old laudanum from Gran's medicine bag—you can't get it for the past quarter century, but Gran kept a small storehouse of such things. This I also mixed with crushed chamomile flower and honey.

And then, at the last moment, feeling too weak to do much about it, I discovered that I'd only enough lavender to stuff one sleeve properly. I thought I'd collected enough over the summer, but the rafters only showed me thyme and rosemary and other such things, and all hung too high for me to get to anymore had I wanted them anyway. My body would not be prepared as well as Gran had prepared hers.

I wondered who might find me, maybe my one surviving brother, maybe my sisters. Maybe someone come up for a salve or a tincture. I wondered whether whoever found me would note the preparation at all. But what matters more: a lavender sleeve half-filled or the hand just under the cuff of that sleeve or the hand just outside it, a hand that's ushered hundreds of babis into this world?

The Weight of Sensible Collections

Gwilym Jones • 1869-1950

Gwilym Jones is my name, Jones the Shop to many, Gwil to a handful of friends. I owned and ran this curio shop—called it the Afar Shoppe—had them put the extra letter 'p' and the extra letter 'e' right there on the sign to give it something special. It cost me more, but was worth it entirely. I like things that set themselves apart. And I was proud to be a merchant, it's a good thing to be. You work hard but get to take your time, and if you feel ill, you can close shop. No man owns you. You stand above many when you're a merchant. So, I enjoyed it entirely, but I loved collecting even more than selling. That can become a problem for a shopkeeper, but I never let it. I kept control of it. Had some level of self-discipline. That said, if you'd the power to come grant my wish or dream, I'd have asked you to make me a top man at a museum—a curator, not a merchant at all. A collector of the highest order. But not you nor I have that power, so a shopkeeper, I am.

Now, if you want to collect, you've got to sell some of what you gather to support the collecting. And you'd want to make a good living, too. So, when I travelled and collected all over the continent, I was always carrying things to sell, here to there, and spot to spot. My delight was mainly curios. That's what thrilled me. But to support that, and to draw in my neighbours, I sold all manner of local sundries in the shop—from farmwives' duck eggs and Welsh cakes to Dai the Saddle's allegedly superior reins and bridles. Still, it was mainly curious things that stuck to me.

My shop, like myself, was never limited by its four walls or by the shape of any island. No, no, I went abroad, and often—at least once a year—a true salesman and a robust sort, too. I had a time alright. Being the sort of body who learned a bit of this language and a bit of that so that I might *fare un bouna fare** as they say in old Italy. Wasn't easy to leave a home with a lovely wife in it, but once I sprung myself free onto the road it was always sure to be a joy. And, besides, too soon into our years, there was no end of sadness at our home. No end of heartbreak. Sadness and heartbreak will do little to keep a man in the house.

I'd leave by wagon and then sea and then train, chugging right across the continent. I was after small things and light things, mainly—curios like I said, and fine, expensive cloth. I hunted Delft and Wode and even Venetian glass, Limoges china and Waterford Crystal, just about like a ferret hunts mink. But I could hardly sell such things here in this village. So, I sold much of it along the way, like I said. Point to point. I might interest a shopkeeper in Paris in a piece of Italian glass or a German in French satin. I might carry money as well, but that's another line of work altogether, light and easy with the possibility of running afoul of the law. Suffice it to say there are side businesses upon side businesses for a traveling merchant, for a man with the gift of gab and a counting sort of mind.

---

*   Make a good or profitable deal

I would always carry home some small treasures to my dear Cranstal, my once-lovely wife. She kept her gifts all about the house and made sure—at least in early days—that they were free from dust or fingerprints. Some I arranged in the front window of the shop as well, to give it an air of finery, which is something that will draw folk in even if they are only after duck eggs and a sack or two of flour. They like to look and wonder. And looking and wondering leads to buying things even if they are other things. For usefulness, I also purchased and shipped home enamel cups and wash-pans, sugar and pickles, oilcloth and scissors, marking chalk, and the like. These my window-shoppers bought. And some of the finer things I hid away knowing they might well increase in value—like money in the bank but better.

There are people who might say that with my love of particularly fine things, I'd have been better off living somewhere else, somewhere on the continent, but I had no interest in leaving my homeland for good—no matter how much I enjoyed travelling in and out of it. I'm simply a migrating sort of man who likes a home to return to, like a stork, I am. Mine was the best shop here, besides the sweet shop, so no proper competition in town. And that's always a good thing for a shopkeeper.

To my eye nothing's more striking than a fine blue and white bone china plate and on it a thin cut of white bread spread with ruby red cherry jam. I might have been an artist in another life. But like I said, the villagers and the country people who timidly came in the shop door did not have eyes trained for delicate things, not mostly. That's why they looked at my best things strangely and then at me strangely. But they were delighted with the sturdier ware, especially squat fireplace spaniels. They were mad for them—for generations. But Cranstal and I never had them in our house.

When I met her, she was called Cranstal Corlett, and she was beautiful. Tall and willowy with long dark hair piled high on the top of her head and a long neck. Her eyes were dark, and the lashes curled up like ebony fans. She had a cleft in her chin, as do I. But hers was just so. When I first saw her I gasped. By the time I was done gasping, I'd already seen in my mind's eye just how all that dark hair and white skin would set off my blue and white porcelain. Oh, I could never help that I was a man who sought beauty. In that moment, I set about courting her.

Like all my best treasures, Cranstal was found over the water. I'd been travelling when I first came upon her looking like a Dutch woman in a painting, as she stood slipping her fingers over the things in her father's Doolish home. I was a handful of years older than her and two fingers shorter, but she didn't mind. She liked me well enough as did her father. I married her and brought her home. And she was no hothouse flower despite her beauty. Cranstal was well able to care for herself when I was away from Nefin on business. Some might say independent, and that would be accurate. I do enjoy people with a bit of independence.

Our son Siôn came within the first year of marriage, and so Cranstal never did travel abroad with me, but she touched the figurines, and dusted them with soft cloths. I do believe she enjoyed them nearly as much as I did. We often would talk about the trips we would take together collecting—later, when all the children we would have were grown. Soon though, we saw our boy Siôn wasn't well and never would be. But we accepted that. As you do. The midwife had noticed first, then Cranstal, but I had refused to believe it for some time. I exercised his infant legs and tried to straighten his body with my hands but gently. Anyone can be wrong, but that time it was me. The condition was not to be cured.

And then we had the girls. Now, they looked healthy enough when they were born, and the midwife said they were. We were in agreement there. You'd think she'd know. Each had dark hair, tiny beginnings of it, and perfect tiny fingernails, and fat little ivory legs with a touch of pink, but besides that they were nondescript, as babies are. But they were ours. Seedling beings, with something to become. Perfect.

When the first one died, some neighbours came to see Cranstal, came to offer up advice about fair folk and what signs to put on our door. Cranstal let them in, and they did the usual things the superstitious do for the *Tylwyth Teg* near and far. There's no land I've travelled to that doesn't have its own version of magical little people. I learned the local lore all too well enough as my old nain kept to such things. I'm a modern man, but we put protections up. Why not? I don't generally hold with nonsense, but even nonsense comes from some sense. And really, I thought to myself back then, what harm is a sign on the door? A splat of dough stuck to the wall? It gave Cranstal some diversion. A placebo, perhaps. But of course, none of it stopped our next baby from dying shortly after her birth. Nor the next. Neither did it stop the fear of the fair family, which had grown like creeping moss in the minds of both my wife and the housekeeper. I should have stopped them, but I'd have had to stay constantly home watching and I had a shop to run.

It was up to me to bury the babies in the garden, left to me to choose a spot near the old dry well. But it had been up to Cranstal that it should ever happen. I shouldn't have put them there, I know that now, but Cranstal was poorly after each one and wanted them where she could see them from the bedroom window on days it was too wet to go out. I should have known they couldn't remain there. I should have known because I'm not a dull man. But I didn't. Or maybe I just couldn't say no.

I had a confession I would never make eating away at me, and it's eating still. When our first baby girl was born, she cried and cried with the colic. I could see it was taking its toll on poor Cranstal. I had seen in my travels the benefits of soothing cordials on infants. There were favourite brands to be sure, but I'd forgotten to think to bring some home with me. And there was no sleep in our house. So, I went to one of my brown envelopes in my dresser drawer and removed one of the ten vials of black opium inside. It was destined for a doctor six towns away who'd not been able to get his shipments on time. He'd never mind if I took a tiny bit. I took an amount the size of the head of a pin, mixed it in a clean empty vial with sugar and water. Dabbed it on the baby's gums. Soon she went to sleep. The next night I did the same with the same effect. I never told Cranstal, and we both slept well for some hours of the night. But when I woke, there was my infant daughter cold and dead. It should have never been enough to kill her, not even to harm her in the least, but still, there she was. I must have made a mistake in my mixing! I must have dipped the pinhead twice! Or three times! One moment I was sure I was to blame. The next, I knew I'd been careful, and it must have been something else. I knew better than to tell Cranstal, for what good would it do any of us.

When the second girl was born, I made sure to say to myself, crying is good. Quiet is a problem. And we were sleepless again, but I would not give her a speck of anything. Wouldn't even rub whiskey on the gums as I'd seen done on every infant from here to Timbuktu. Cranstal, again, was exhausted. As was I. But I had to get up to run the shop in the mornings and could not snatch bits of sleep when the baby piped down. So, a few nights I stumbled out the door and went to sleep in the shop for a while—drove down and back up before the sun. And then back again to open the shop, the horse as tired as me and stumbling.

On Sundays, the shop was closed. And so, on a Sunday after capel, I thought I might take over with the little baby girl for the day and let Cranstal sleep. She was in great need of rest, but she paced and worried so. I made her tea, and I went to my little opium vial—which I'd kept back from the doctor—having delivered him only nine—and put a bit in her tea. Just a little. No more than would have let me sleep well on a train hurtling from distant station to distant station. She was a grown body, and I knew what I was doing. I knew it would help. And I knew if she didn't get some sleep, Cranstal might well fall ill. It worked like a charm, and I found that if I gave her just the tiniest amount in her tea she would not fall asleep but simply not panic about the baby's cries. Live with it calmly. So, I brewed her a tea in the morning, a tea when I came back from the shop, and another before we went to bed. Just a speck of opium in each. As Cranstal calmed, so did the baby. I thought perhaps it had been Cranstal's nervousness making the little thing squall. After all, poor Cranstal hadn't had an easy time of mothering since the start. But then we found poor little Esyllt dead in her cradle.

Had it come into her milk? Was it possible? Had I killed another one of my children? Who can tell his wife such a thing? Who can tell anyone? Who can even let himself believe his own stupidity? Perhaps a better man than I. For I convinced myself it was, indeed, cot death. For there is such a thing as cot death. But I also doubted myself.

When the third tiny girl died, well, I'd not put a drop of anything in anything. In fact, I had stayed as far away from both wife and tiny daughter as possible, and still she died the same way. I started to think it was because of the other two. I started to feel there was a big finger of the universe pointing at me—the culprit of the other two. And through them, of this last one, as well. That I deserved the third death. That my guilt had brought it on. That I was the cause of all catastrophe through my meddling. I was never a man prone to these sorts of thoughts, or any sort of lack of confidence, but I found myself, in those years, dancing on the brink of madness whilst running a shop—with no one the wiser. I was going invisibly mad. Most days I hated myself. And in my madness, I found myself even more unable to say no to Cranstal about anything. She got her way with all the babies—I buried them as she directed. I kept my mouth shut. I felt it would be my penance to have to step over them in the garden, to be reminded night and day of what I'd probably caused.

And then, when Cranstal truly lost her mind from looking down on them day and night, it was up to me to move them. I had to come to my senses. For all our sakes.

The day I did it, she stared out the window like a certified lunatic. I had Yolanda give her some opium in her tea. No harm now. Then I set to work digging them up like tulip bulbs, precious. And carefully I moved them to a proper spot for infants, in the old cemetery. A few neighbours helped, strong men with shovels, Huw Priddy and Evans the Pig, Dai the Saddle. It was with the blessings of their wives, who agreed that it must be done and sent them out their doors with flasks of tea. And we worked until what needed to be done was done. I thought we might start anew. Begin again. Find peace with the problem moved. Reconsider the possibility that it had been cot death all along. Or what the doctor in town much later described to me as a 'congenital abnormality.'

But there was no bringing Cranstal to a clean slate. She left me. Not right away. In fact, I should say, at first, she seemed to improve. I was certain, then, I'd done the right thing in moving the babies to the old graveyard. Look how she's flowering, I thought to myself. I felt proud and manly in myself that I'd taken charge and righted the situation. That I'd saved her from the compounding grief. But her recovery, it was only a ruse. She waited until I was out of the house and over the cliff she went. Some days I was sure she jumped. And others I talked myself into a certainty that she'd only slipped, that she wouldn't have left me here all alone but for Siôn. The footpath on a wet day can be treacherous. Or maybe it was that she allowed herself to slip. It's a fine line between the two, flinging yourself over and allowing it to simply happen. But slowly I came to know that, like a great many things in this world and beyond, there's a more confounding truth, and that's the truth of knowing you will never know the truth. What I do know is that I made hideous mistakes. And not one of them could be righted.

When they carried her wet body home to me, she was so unrecognisable I let myself hope for a moment that it wasn't her. But as it was wearing her clothes, I had to silence the mad storytelling in my head. I had to make decisions. Of course, I had momentary thoughts. Thoughts to make amends by burying Cranstal at home, right where the babies had once been. And then to bring the babies back, too. But I thought better of it. So, into the old, old graveyard I put my dear Cranstal, next to the babies, just up the cliff from the sea into which she fell. And I never went up there again.

Now, ONCE I'D LOST Cranstal, I determined I was done with having a wife, with having more children, all that. I could bear no more. It wasn't like I had a brood that needed mothering. Just Siôn. So, the housekeeper, Yolanda, stayed on to care for Siôn, and I put my mind into the shop and not much else. Perhaps, in time, I'd have remembered my love for Siôn and found solace there, been the best father to a broken boy, made him my life. But too soon I had no children at all. Siôn had never been strong, you see. My children, it seems, were not for this life. And perhaps, because of it, they escaped no small amount of suffering. Now I had no one to worry over.

People narrowed their eyes at Yolanda, particularly when she stayed on after Siôn died. Let them think what they like. Yolanda was never my lover. God knows, I needed to leave that place, this whole place, sometimes. I needed to do my work. I had a business to run. And you know what? Yolanda made good, hearty victuals on cold nights and kept things tidy and dry. And she knew numbers—could keep records on a ledger in her way. She was useful and good tempered. But neighbours stopped sending fairy signs and well-wishes. In chapel, they moved away from Yolanda when she sat down, and my business suffered and a new shop opened up, not nearly as fine as mine. The son of Evans the Box, who should have stuck with coffins, and who liked to put his finger on the scales. But since the village had decided against me and Yolanda, they preferred him.

No matter, Gwilym Jones is not a man to be put out of business by the cold shoulder, so every market Saturday, Yolanda and I, we closed the shop and loaded up a cart of carefully packed goods and drove three villages down the coast to a town with no shop at all. The people there were happy to buy from us. Truly, the whole thing was no hair off my back. All along, through it all, I still went abroad making deals, and only on the road was I able to put down my troubles.

On the days we moved shop to the far-off town, Yolanda and I would pack the night before, using every blanket and remnant of cloth in the shop and the house to keep things from rattling. And then I'd drive the winding roads very slowly so as not to break a piece. For years, we did that, until people started coming to the shop again, as people do when they find the other shopkeeper has been up to worse. Apparently, young Evans the Box had been seen slapping his own shouting mother through his home window by a passer-by. In a trice, we were now the favourite and he was driven out of business as there's little worse you can do than to put hands on your own mam. And he went back to coffins.

In time, business increased beyond where it had been to start. Times changed. People earned just a little more money, and tourists flocked in greater numbers. They're an annoying bunch in general if you forget to take into account they've got some money to spend. And they wanted local items, 'primitive art,' not Limoges or Waterford. If they'd wanted those, they'd have headed out to Limoges or Waterford and not come to North Wales. No, they wanted what we have naturally. So, I had to leave my fine things in the storeroom collecting dust and increase my buying up local ware from an old man's fire kiln and woollen shawls knitted by bent-armed grannies. That sort of thing. I conscripted big Aggie Monroe into making generations of little dolls from their place up on the hill. And I didn't just put the dolls and coarse jars on a shelf. No, I *displayed* them. Yolanda laughed when we closed the doors at night, and smiled when we counted the money. Yet, despite the good feeling of a sale, I couldn't take real pleasure in the items. The muted colours, their rough textures. They were not pleasing to my eye. It was the same as how I couldn't take pleasure in Yolanda who was also muted and somewhat rough and sturdy. I knew well she was on offer, and I'd have been counted lucky by many to have a woman such as her. But the heart will have what it wants, they say, and just as sure, it will not have what it doesn't want. I wanted Cranstal still and always.

And that's where we stuck—Yolanda my helper, never my lover. Me trading locally into old age. The vial of opium burned up in the hearth in a rage one night—a night I determined whether I should take it all myself and end my guilt along with my life or just end my guilt *without* dying. I started making friends here and there as those who shunned me went marching into their graves. I went all the way to the National Library in Aberystwyth and researched cot death and congenital abnormalities in medical magazines. I remembered how I used to let Lili Morgan use the shop as a library—giving her fashion magazines to read, encouraging her ambition. That girl, though no kin of mine, had reminded me so much of myself—and she was near the age my eldest daughter would have been. How I'd enjoyed her quiet presence in the shop—her good eye—until she ran off to London. Good fortune to her. The Morgans will say that she went off to help some maiden aunt in Glamorgan, but it's unlikely. She'd have returned eventually. Maiden aunts don't live forever. It might be that old Morgan just couldn't stand the shame of his daughter having run off on her own. Couldn't stand the independence in her. I thought on that quite a bit over the years and that's where I've arrived. Given my history of losing daughters, I suppose I'm finely attuned to such things. Anyway, decades and decades passed without a sighting of Lili Morgan though I never stopped wondering about her.

When my heart started beating off beats, during my eightieth year, I carried the little music box that was Cranstal's down to the shop. A pretty little thing I'd given Cranstal on our wedding day. I allowed myself to wind it twice a day, at opening and at closing but no more so that I didn't bog down in it. Old age may well be reserved for the sentimental, but you can't just let it have its way. Sometimes, at home, I dreamed that I heard rocking cradles, and I knew well it was only because Cranstal had put that in my head so long ago. My sleep was not restful. And so, I'd taken to sleeping on a cot, back of the storeroom at the shop, a few nights a week. Easier not going back and forth every day, and Yolanda kept a close eye on the house anyway.

THE DAY I DIED, I sipped black tea in the shop early in the morning and nibbled half a cake Mrs. Evans the Box had brought in to sell. Generally, I wouldn't behave like that, eating up the profits, but I was ravenous and my rheumatism was giving me a lot of pain. I put my coin in for it and wrapped the other half in a tea cloth to be sold as a half-cake. I wound the little box and listened while I ambled around feather dusting all the glass things up on the front shelves where spiders had been having their way that summer. The music was tinkling as I turned over the open sign. I checked the till for adequate change. Having already broken my own rules about eating cakes for sale, I also broke my two-wind rule and set the music box to playing a second and then a third time as I waited for old Huw Priddy to come by for a swig with me. I expected he'd come banging in the door asking, like always, '*Beth sydd ar y gweill?*'* What's knitting on the needles, man? And I'd have some small or large news for him about who'd been recently in and out the shop and so on. Not *gossip*, mind you, just happenings. There was something in the air about Evans the Box's grandson and the law. We liked to talk over our work. We'd been onto fossils lately, and it wasn't just something to keep us occupied. Great demand for fossils these days and that kept a spark to me. I was looking forward to holding up the magnifying glass and having good talk.

But then, just as I was about open the door and tell him what was up, the shop walls went all sideways and curvy like a rippled pond, so I lay down on the wooden floor so as not to break anything on the shelves if I should fall. He let himself in and said to me, 'are you alright, friend?'

'Not so great at the moment,' said I.

And there I died knowing well that Priddy would handle it in the right way. You don't want to die in front of just anyone. I knew

----

* What's up?

he'd do right by me. Close my eyes, fix me up, make sure I was put in at the old cemetery with Siôn and Elen and Eysllt and Baby and with lovely Cranstal. Where I belonged and where I could lay down and sleep. We would all be the same now.

The Substance of a Good Home

Aggie Monroe • 1871-1959

I won't speak to you about being dead. Nor about the act of dying. It strikes me as a dull topic altogether. Though I suppose I might have to at the end. For you'll be wondering. People do like to know. But for me, *life* was all. And life was so much more than death could ever be. Life made me laugh and feel strong. Now, many hereabouts would say to you, 'Oh, that Aggie Monroe? Who was *she* to laugh at anything? What kind of life did *she* have? That big old spinster. How sad, a woman with no man and no child to call her own.'

But they didn't know much. I'd no husband because I wanted no husband. I swear on the Good Book, it's true. And besides, since no man came calling for me, I was doubly blessed by being spared the tiresome chore of refusing one. I've heard that there are men unlikely to take the news in their stride.

Yes, I escaped that neatly, didn't I?

Because I never married like my older sisters did, nor went out for service like my younger, I remained at home with my elders, caring for them. There was her, mild as milk, and him one crusty cock-of-the-walk, strutting under his cap, pipe clenched in his teeth, poking his nose here and there. The old man came from what he liked to say was 'good family.' One with nary a teetotaller nor a drunkard among them. 'Monroes,' he said, 'were as near to God's wish as could be found.'

Mam, though, when he'd finished, would whisper after him, 'But not *the mother*. See how he won't mention his mother in that godly lot? Listen and you'll never hear the name of her.'

Now, Mam and Dat weren't much for bickering, and that was good, for living with bickering parents is a burden that would have sent me straight out of the house. No, they never bickered. Instead, he said his piece and then, when he left the room, she said hers.

I was the second to youngest child in a clutch of wilful girls. So Mam and Dat were both soft-worn and prone to napping by the time I was left alone with them, my older sisters having all flown into marriage, and Yolanda having gone down to the Joneses.

I loved the two old dears, even him with his stand-up hair and beady eye. And speaking of the hair and eye, I must admit I inherited both. The three of us spent many a night together, him holding forth by the fire on one ancient war or another. In a *lather* over the English having done such and such a thing. For wasn't he a Welshman? And then in a *lather* at the Welsh for having done some other thing. For wasn't he a subject of the crown? In my Dat's eyes, no one ever was in the right, it seemed. There was always a new argument to be had.

He had once been the schoolmaster, and so an expert in arguments of all sorts. The good old *dissoi-logi*, he called it. And that, he said is from the Greek. It means to have the ability to argue both sides of any argument given. And having been relieved of his school teaching, he continued teaching at our fireside most nights. That was the general thing, him lecturing and her asking if we wouldn't just like another cup or a cut of bread with butter with a boiled egg on top. And what was I doing? Sitting quietly and nodding? Ignoring him? No, I was nearly always arguing against him in some way. For I'd not learned Mam's gentle manner of disagreement. Nor did I want to.

My father and I kept our beady eyes fixed on one another. Though we often turned as if to look out the window—as if we didn't care a whit—while we stalked around the room. Always railing over politics and ideas and histories—him pronouncing me a traitor to Wales in front of the burning hearth. For I saw great good in the Irish and some good in the English I knew. And then soon after, he'd pronounce me a traitor to the crown. How his hand raked his hair in contempt, leaving it somehow wilder. And yet he smiled out the window, for he did love to hold forth with me in the house. A sparring partner worthy of a nightly bout.

By the time I reached my middle thirties, though, they were both dead and gone. Him first, and then her, quickly after, as if she were chasing him down, afraid he'd lecture in heaven without her to quietly set it straight when he left the room.

When there are seven daughters and one home, there's no fair way to divide things. So, the old man and woman left me the house and bit of land it sits upon, for my troubles. Me having stayed home with them the longest. The others got trinkets, and I got real property. I got home.

I leave it to you to imagine how *that* went over. It's not uncommon.

It's a small place, a cottage really. But sturdy with thick stone walls and all the windows facing the right direction, toward the milder breezes and sunshine of the south slope of the mountain here. It's hard to tell when the air is still like it is tonight, but come wintertime, you'll soon learn the difference between a south breeze and a north wind!

There's a tiny henhouse up the small knob hill that rises like a little head on top of the main hill, for chickens and ducks. And there are two fine, green pastures for sheep, which I let a man keep, and which he paid me rent on. That brought in a little extra. I had a long ten years by myself to think over my own life and theirs in this house. And bits of them and of all my sisters as children followed me about and kept me company if I got lonely. But truth be told, I don't mind in the least being on my own in such a snug place. It's nice to come and go as you please. To sit up late as you like. To sleep in late when you like. You see enough people between capel and shop not to get lonely.

I was not wealthy, though, despite the cottage and the let on the fields. And sometimes I worried I might lose the place if I didn't get some money coming in. But then I had some luck on the hottest night of the year. It was an unseasonable burner of a night, and I was getting to that age where I sometimes felt I'd burn up even in the cool weather. So, I was pink as a roasting gammon and naked as a new-hatched robin. I determined that the only help for me was to get up and flip the heavy mattress over to its cool side. Now, I was hot at work, wrestling it up against the wall—as you must when flipping a mattress in tight quarters—when I heard the chink-chink of coins falling inside. Nothing but coins sound like coins, and quick, I ran to the kitchen for a knife to release them. I gutted that mattress like a trout.

Up to my armpits in goose feathers, I touched the first two coins in a pool of them that had shaken together. I remained in a sweat fishing for coins till dawn—for some of them were very stubborn and seemed to retreat from my stretching fingers. But I had to get every last one out. I noted my good fortune and thanked my departed, frugal parents, as well as the hot night that caused me to turn the mattress, I thanked them all with each coin I plucked from the ticking. And when I was certain I'd captured the lot, I sewed the old mattress back up with strong red yarn, pulling the stitches tight until it was good as ever. For a real mattress is a thing of great value.

It was hard to get back to sleep.

The next morning, I glugged down my tea, dressed, and set out directly for the Post Office. The coins were like ship's ballast in my hip pockets. Into that Post Office, I marched, clinking with each step. Onto the counter it all went. Price the Eyebrow was manning the counter, bald-headed clerk with one raised long brown eyebrow spanning his entire forehead like a prostrated ferret. He'd once been Price the Post, but he'd recently been upgraded in both name and position.

'And where did this come from, Aggie?'

I said to him, without a blink—for I never much liked being questioned—'And wouldn't you like to know?'

'Well, then,' he said, and nothing more. He stamped my book, stacking my coins.

'Well then, what?' said I, looking him in the eye.

He pursed his lips and continued stamping.

My pile of coins—neither pittance nor great fortune—would be handsome enough to carry me happily for years, and it irked me to hand it to Price. But I'm a modern sort, and I do believe the Post Office is the best place for money. Not the mattress, nor the cake tin, nor the hole in the wall. For aren't those surely the first places a thief is bound to look? Any hidey-hole you can think to stash away a treasure, a thousand thieves have already thought it themselves. A body can drive itself mad attempting to find the perfect hiding place, putting the coins in, then taking them out again. Like a rat scurrying about with a duck's egg! I should know as I'd tried it myself during the night.

So Price and his eyebrow finished stamping my ledger book and I went home to a cool mattress with the bright red yarn stitch, like a glorious scar. And I had a fine sleep. Mind you, it's not that I truly trusted the banks and post offices and such, no, and no one *should*. But what are the choices? The thing with money is common sense, and I possessed more than my share of that good thing. I could hold forth like Dat on common sense—it's similar to money. But I'll not bore you, except to say, if you have none, you *will* suffer, and if you do have some, you will suffer less in certain ways.

Part of common sense is to develop a skill or two that will make you useful in the world. The world is full of useless people. And it's best not to join their ever-swelling ranks. I was once very good at tatting lace and general sewing. And I made a bit extra at that. But then, in the years after the war, tourists started coming to Wales like a blessed plague. And it was then I was struck by a genius idea. Dolls.

And so, I began making dolls, though as a girl I'd cared not a whit for them, preferring jumping and walking along the tops of stone walls. I may have never played with one, but I certainly cottoned on quickly to how to make a good doll. Fabric dolls, all done up in the costume of days gone by. They were clever and droll, and simply made. The more homely they were, the more the tourists bought. Jones the Shop called my dolls 'primitive art' and agreed to sell them in the front, where he kept woolen blankets and clay cups. And to send them in crates to his contacts in the south. My dollies sold so fast that Jones was seen, regularly, clomping up the hill to this house to ask if I couldn't make more, and make them faster. In the summer months, there was no keeping Jones in dolls, though I did my best. I found great pleasure in making dolls, and equally or more so, in marching up to the post office and pushing more coins at Price behind the counter.

It must be that I made thousands of dolls, each just a bit different from the last: a lopsided eye, or a wriggled smile, maybe a new colour in the *betgwn** and shawl for the doll women. The men were dressed with whatever remnants there were. And so, their jackets matched and that made it easy to keep pairs together. When I finished with each doll, it was always a curious thing to see what I had turned out. And an even curiouser thing to feel a pinch of sadness as I stuffed them into a wooden crate to go off to the shop and then out into the wide world. It was just a tiny pinch, though, because I knew it to be silly. And Aggie Monroe never was given to silliness. I had to laugh at myself, have a cup, and start the next dolly.

At first, I gathered the wool to stuff them from what I discovered stuck to the thistles and fence wire in the pasture. And there were masses of it to gather and I so enjoyed taking long walks across the sheep fields to the edge of the cliff, though it always made me sad to remember it was just there that Cranstal Jones went over, rest her soul. I couldn't dwell on it though. Too sad.

I used the gathered tufts only to stuff the dollies. Not for carding and spinning, weaving and dyeing. That would be an altogether foolish amount of work. Tourists do swoon for the homespun. For the blood, sweat, and tears. But I'd not the time for that nonsense. And tourists don't need to know if you *aren't* plucking wool from thistles for the little skirts and capes. Let them imagine what they will.

What I used for years were old clothes. I went into cupboards and boxes left behind, and I cut Mam and Dat's clothes to pieces. That's what I did, to make the dolls' clothes. Until I ran out, which took some time, for doll's clothes are very small. Yes, indeed, I put my father's trousers and my mother's second best and third best dress, and her woolies, too, out into the world on the backs and fronts of dolls. It was the best use of things.

---

*   Gown

Once I'd sewn the last bit of Mam's last dress—a blue and green house dress—onto a tribe of black-eyed dollies, I got Jones to save me remnants of woolen bolts from his shop. And I used those. He took an extra ten percent of my profits in return, and that was fair enough.

Now, I must confess that I knew Jones the Shop was carrying on with my younger sister, Yolanda. And he had been for years. There's no delicate way to put such an indelicate situation. A situation that made Jones especially willing to sell my wares. As if he had something to atone for. I'd had Yolanda put in a good word for me, here and there, and why not? It was her business, entirely, and the world is full of unusual arrangements if you look closely. I never did hold it against her, the arrangement she had with Jones.

Mam and Dat, though, God rest them, they did. Particularly Dat. And right up to and including the day he died. Mam said it was because his own mother had that red hair, and she was wild, too, so he knew what sort of creature he was dealing with in his youngest daughter. But Dat always said it was Mam who made her so, by giving her such an exotic name. When he said so, Mam pretended she couldn't hear him and told me later, in a corner, that there'd been no such behavior in *her* family, where the name came from. What's more—and never spoken of—is the fact that no matter how Dat tried to teach her when she was little, Yolanda would never learn to read. She couldn't hardly tell an A from an F. Numbers she could do, but letters, never. And more the shame for him, a schoolteacher. He thought she did it just to spite him. But about that he was wrong. She just could not do it. And she began to cease to exist for him even then, long before she ever knew Jones or his wife.

But once he heard the sordid tale of Yolanda and Jones, Dat's mobile mouth stopped up the moment any conversation came to Yolanda. I reckon he'd heard the gossip, trotting around town as it did. Our dat, upon her shaming, conspired with himself to stroll past her, as if without *seeing her* at all. If she called out to him, and she did regularly for the first while, his pace never slowed by even a fraction. His breathing never changed. It was like he was a wizard who could make her vanish from the very middle of the road or from the pew or from the doorstep. It made me sad for Yolanda, but there was nothing I could do then; though when the old man and old woman were gone, I shared some of the coins with Yolanda, here and there. When she was in need, but not too regular. For didn't she live in Jones's house, with the lovely cupboards and bursting larder? And her Jones's own darling now, no matter how she denied it to me?

But who were any of us to judge Yolanda? It was *bound* to happen. My sister was a stunner, and Jones the Shop a lonely man with a very sick wife, and then with no wife at all. I'd not have been interested in Gwilym Jones myself, but then I was never that way for the men. I look at them without a speck of passion. Now, Jones was pleasant enough in that stocky of body, side parted hair, ever-earnest expression sort of way. He smelled of Bay Rum, and behind his ears was clean. He had little blonde hairs on his knuckles and red ones in his beard, which was short and neatly trimmed for most of his life. A beard that made you just *know* he wanted to look like Errol Flynn though he hadn't the build for it. I knew Gwilym Jones all of his life. I looked closely at him, body and spirit, trying to see what drew Yolanda. And sure enough, my sister gave up any other prospects for him, a kind and polite red calf in a middling suit with a shop.

Thank God she never did become pregnant, I used to think. But now I wish she had. That would have at least brought things to a head. I think she must have been barren. Some in town believe the Jones place is cursed by the fair family. Too many dead children, and barren Yolanda to top it off. Some at capel say her barrenness is a punishment from God on high—for fornication, adultery and general sinfulness. I find that idea foolish. God seldom punishes adulterers with barrenness from what I've seen and heard. Why my sister never had a child, I cannot say. Though I doubt God nor the fairies were responsible. I'm one for science.

Whatever the cause, there was my poor sister, who had always wanted a husband and children, with neither. And there had been poor Cranstal Jones and her dead babis. And that bent-up little boy, too. What a place that was. But I never let Yolanda's troubles cost me a night's sleep, nor those of Alys, nor Ellie, nor Mari. Not Perla nor Harriet, either. I'd too many sisters to start that sort of worry—if I'd begun, there'd have been no end to it. And besides, I had my own gorgeous life to keep my eyes on. And *gorgeous* it was, for *I* knew happiness.

My Aderwen moved up into the house. Into *our* house, with the south facing windows and the slant sun, one day when I was busy sewing a pack of particularly round-headed dolls. We were the same age and had been schoolgirls together. And there we were, suddenly face to face again: me a spinster and her a runaway wife of forty-five. That's how we stood, facing one another on the day she dropped her embroidered bag and umbrella on my sitting room floor. She was still as beautiful as ever though her black curls were tinged with grey now, like a scant dusting of snow had landed on her. And her cheeks red from the walk up the hill. Here was my friend who came with only a bag, an umbrella, and her troubles, of course. But her troubles were safe with me.

My Aderwen never asked, 'Can I stay?' I never thought to ask her if she would. The likes of the two of us don't need to ask such things.

She stayed. And we planted a drift of sweet violets on the shady side of the house, and kept potted African sorts in the big casement that spring. And the next and the next and the next. We decided we were the queens of violets, and there was no end to our violet dividing and planting. For we simply adored them, with their little clown's faces and sweet nectar.

We both wore our hair in high knots and let the wisps or curls fall where they would—I had wisps, and she, lovely curls. Aderwen had no interest in making dollies, so she kept house while I sewed. I bent over the woolen faces, French knotting the black eyes tight to their heads. She bent over some hot soup pot or scrubbed the table top clean as a bone—or else she just stared quietly into the fire. We stopped regularly for tea and honey, and on the cold days, a drop of whiskey by that fire.

While we sat, I told her old stories of Mam and Dat, and of their peculiarities. And then of all the things that were going on in the village, the countryside, and in the world. For didn't I subscribe to the *Baner ac Amserau Cymru** and read it regular? I did. Though it often took Jones some time to get it to me, and the news might be a tad stale. No matter, we enjoyed it, and I read it aloud for Aderwen, who was never a strong reader back in our school days. Her eyes were always a bit weak. So, there we sat, just there, in our chairs by the fire. Our days were simple, and they ran together. We took to smoking pipes like fiends soon after she arrived.

MY ADERWEN CREPT INTO my own bed one night when the fire went out and we'd forgotten to bring in wood to dry. A night without a moon, but somehow, her dressing gown glowed as she came across the flag floor. She crawled into my bed, shivering but trying not to. I pretended to be asleep for a while, a long while. I barely breathed. She held her breath, too; I could tell. We inched closer

---

*   *Flag and Times of Wales*

bit by bit by bit. In the pure darkness, we did embrace. And kiss. Her feet were cold and smooth.

Each and every day, Aderwen would say to me, while tucking some stray curl behind her ear, 'Today won't be coming back, not ever.' Sometimes, I didn't want to hear that. So, I ignored her. Told her to shush. For surely, she was wasting the time we had by worrying about the end. But most times, I just nodded because it *was* true and because I didn't like to hurt her feelings. Or to feel sad in myself. I suppose I could have cried because my Aderwen, who I loved best of all people in this world, and who I loved longest as well, was sad in herself. Such a gift she was to me. *And* a surprise. But if I were to start crying, I might not dry up again. What a sight that would have been—me bawling in my chair, dolls strewn all about. Like they say, there's no fool like an old fool.

And besides, one thing about Aderwen was this: if someone cried, *she* cried. Be it an old man, a school teacher, a babi, or a shrieking piglet, she didn't mind. She was cry for cry, my Aderwen. No, it would never do for me to shed a tear and start it all off.

So, I listened to Aderwen say that same dear thing to my back as I sat in my chair nearly every day for forty-odd years. Always in her same voice, full and whispery. Aderwen had been known by all for the beautiful voice she had—when she wasn't too shy to talk. And that voice never abandoned her throat. But once she came here, no one but me heard it.

We got old. Like you will. It wasn't a shock and it took some time. But it *was* something of a surprise. Still. We lived longer than many our age, longer than that blackguard down the hill, Twm… I promised Aderwen I wouldn't name him. But there I've gone and done it. Old Aggie Monroe was never known for her closed mouth, I wasn't. And I don't see much use in hiding the sins of others, but I won't say more on that—I promise. Oh, how I struggle to hold my battering ram of a tongue. Even now.

As I was saying, we got old. The neighbours started nosing about, like a small army of nurses, bringing warmish soup and looking to see if we had thick enough blankets and a store of firewood to keep us.

'And where is Aderwen's bed,' they asked?

'Long gone,' I told them.

'Why's that?' they asked.

'What's it to you?' I said.

'Well, it's just that you might be spreading germs breathing all over each other,' said a tall one, a bit too loudly. I can't remember if she came from up or down the lane, but I'd seen her before. She leaned against the AGA, taking its heat, and added 'We have only your best interests at heart.'

'Aggie's got no germ!' shouted Aderwen from where they'd put her on the sofa, 'no germs on Ag!'

It was the only thing she'd said since they'd barged in, and the lot of them looked over in surprise. And her surprised, too. Aderwen's white hair was down, wild as her eyes, her blue nightgown rumpled up across her knees. They tried to get her to say more, but she was done with it. Other than her mumbling, which they could not fathom a blue word of. I knew she was quietly inventing curses never before heard in the countryside—crumble arse jumblers, and biting bastard bluflers—the like of *that*. Aderwen had a gift with the curse.

'And why does Aderwen mumble so?' they wanted to know.

'And when was the last time those curtains was washed? Too dusty by a sight. Have any of you ever seen curtains so dusty as that? And are you needing anyone to go to the Post Office for a withdrawal? Or to market?'

On and on and on they went, offering things of which we had neither want nor need. I still did all of that myself. And Aderwen sat patiently by the fire, waiting for me to return on the days I went into the village. I told them to scatter to the winds. We'd send word if we needed them. For didn't we have a telephone right there on the wall?

That one with the familiar face, she had a retort. She said to me, 'and do I have a telephone on *my* wall? How can you possibly phone me without a telephone on *my* wall?'

She wore frustration at her nose like a bull's ring, and anyone could see it. 'No, Aggie Monroe, my own wall sports no telephone. So what good does yours do, Aggie Monroe? Yes, you've got new hob—an AGA at that—and *telephone*, but the rest of us haven't got any of that. That's why we've got to hoof up your bloody hill to check on you. And you don't appreciate it in the least. You are one angry woman, *Angry* Monroe.'

'I am *now*,' I said. 'As I look at you!' I knew I was playing the part, but sometimes it's the only way. I wanted them gone.

'Now, why don't you scatter! We can do without you!'

Aderwen grumbled in agreement, and the do-gooders huffed out of my house. I wondered who had set them upon us. Likely the capel folk, meaning well enough. I was proud of myself that I still had the huff and puff left in me to drive them out, like a young bitch after sheep. I got up to open the front door a crack so I could stand in the frame and watch them pick their way back down to the road. They stumbled and slipped on the many loose stones on the path, as we had not been up to keeping it neat. While they were still in range of hearing, I *slammed* the door. 'Good riddance!'

Aderwen and I had tea with no sugar and no honey. For, indeed, we needed things from the market. We smoked our pipes, and worried they'd be back too soon. Fine rain tinked against the pane, and we felt snug enough for a while.

Not long after, came the time I *needed* their help. After Aderwen fell next to the bed. She'd tripped over my slippers and went down flat on her face. There was blood from her nose. My fault. I couldn't get her back up on my own. So, I lurched down the hill, slowly now, for I was truly old. And that was the day, standing on my floor quite confident, one of them asked, 'And shouldn't you have someone come out to stay, shouldn't you, *really*?'

Oh, that worried voice was shrill. As if the breath crowded and stuck inside her nostrils. I said no, we needed no one in our home. We were well enough so long as I kicked my slippers *under* the bed. And if they'd just get her up off the floor, that was all the help we needed.

They hoisted poor Aderwen up and set her in her fireside chair. Checked her for bruises. They held out their fingers in front of her face and asked her to count them. She refused. 'Out,' I said, 'Out!' I'm not always so rude, but they had a *roosting* look about them. They craned their necks, looking at me over their shoulders and went too slowly for the door. The one tucked black curls behind her ear. Same as Aderwen does. I couldn't be sure at the time. But Aderwen and I think, now, it was her own Edna. Could well have been. Our eyes were too dim to be certain, and you can't ask a question like that without knowing the answer beforehand. Especially considering what had passed between Aderwen and her young ones. No, Aderwen couldn't ask. And she didn't want me to either.

But I've been talking a long time, haven't I? And really it's Aderwen's turn now. I'm surprised I've told you so much here in the light of the moon. Aderwen believes the full moon makes even the most practical among us talk too much. I don't set much store by superstitions, but she insists. No matter, I've told you my story, if it's a story at all. I like to think it's *not*. It's simply a life. And there's not much that comes in above life. All else I will say is this.

Aderwen and I, we were lovely up to the last. Which came soon after Aderwen fell over my slippers the second time again. No one can say otherwise of us, and if they did, we wouldn't care a whit anyhow.

We're still here, and the drift of sweet violets we planted long ago still blooms, even in the night, doesn't it?

The Implications of Remembering

Aderwen • 1871-1959

W on't use my married name. No, told Aggie that before I agreed to speak. It's a condition of it. Speaking, that is. Speaking to you especially. It's nothing about you though—nothing against you, just so you know. Just that you're a stranger. And just that I've always been quiet like my dat. Like his mam before him. Not timid. Not shy. That other sort of quiet. So quiet some people thought me simple. Some folk are just made quiet. Like some are made loud. Though I say it's easier for loud ones to be quiet than for quiet ones to be loud.

I'd rather have pulled weeds than opened my mouth in choir. Rather have sat down for supper with one soul than with ten. And happy I was pulling weeds among the cabbages or sitting fireside with my pipe's smoke curling in shapes overhead. Just watching the flames dance in the hearth.

Now, Aggie—there's a talker, born and bred. And smarter than anyone you'll meet. Trust her, I do. Aggie's never let me down, nor really anyone else. She's a dependable woman. Which is good because it's just us here together now. But not like before. No, not like that. Because it's *dead* we are now.

Dead, achan! Can you credit it?

Aggie can. Ag says, now you're dead, Aderwen, no need to be hush-mouthed. Say what you have to say for once. See how it feels finally. Says give it a good try Aderwen, now that your mind is back to itself. So, here I am now, giving it a good try. I know Ag's right, but she's also a bit *bossy*, God love her. But she promised not to interrupt, so she's right here beside me, staying quiet as she can.

Truth is, I'm still confused sometimes. Just don't know what to make of how we are now. And me still coming back from forgetful. From old age when I misplaced whole months. Lost stockings, needles, pipe, mislaid specs. There we were then, crawling around to find things, and me forgetting what we were looking for during the crawl.

Even forgot what's *onions*.

Even forgot how to speak.

Forgetting, though, wasn't all bad. Forgot many troubles too, forgot all about my life down the hill, once with a husband and children. Before I came to Aggie's. Instead, there were days when only girlhood sights and sounds came through. Like how once a lone goose flew over me, orange paddle feet hanging down, back when I was seven. Then, there I was, under the goose instead of in my chair by the fire, though I could feel the heat singeing my shins. Sometimes my memories put me down under Mam's kitchen table with the little dog, watching it chew the table leg. I was four, and I hid with a little square of bara brith. Must have been a special day, for we seldom had treats. Down there with all the chew marks the dog made when she was a pup, I gave her some of my raisin bits and she licked them from my finger tip. Old memories had me stuck. Feels queer *knowing* now-things again. Like blood coming back into a leg fallen asleep from too long sitting wrong.

Tell you all about our Aggie, now. Yes, I'd like to, and since it's my turn I will. Was a tall freckle-face, freckle-arm girl, Ag. Eyes on her sharp as a crow's. Shared her food with me most days when we were small girls, as her mam kept hen and cow alike. Aggie was queen of boiled eggs, near all she wanted. And queen of milk, too. Even cream on occasion. Her dat had been school teacher before he fell wrong side of the local council. After that he spent most of his time indoors, writing up speeches for others, solicitors and mayors and such, who would never admit they didn't write their own. Was paid some. But no one was to know this back then.

Wasn't paid much, though. So was Ag's mam kept the holding going, her and Ag's sisters. Ag, too. Each a job to do, creature to tend, bread to bake and bring to market. Like clockwork, those Monroe women. No eggs of my own living at home with my big sis Aberfa. Only greens and porridge with a rabbit here and there. Winkles sometimes. And snails. Any milk did come from our bony cow went to babis. And when the cow died, well, that was the end of that. Greens growed out the back plus turnips, cabbages, swedes. We did our best, but it was never enough. Can't fault Aberfa. 'Fact can't fault none for not having. Aberfa most of all. Her worn thin as slate by babis, babis, babis, one after another.

Was living with Aberfa and her man because Mam, then Dat, had died one after the other. No money for doctor means folk go quick to the grave. And it's not unusual. What took Mam and Dat and some Evans down by the sea as well as some Williams up mountainside was no more than some such common sickness as was always sweeping broom across the countryside. Sweeping people off away like they were no more than dust already.

So, there was I, eight-year-old orphan with a sister for mam. And *her* so clean tired she'd never pack me a dinner to have at school, even if there *was* something to put in it. So I didn't trouble her asking. Dinner is for the well-off. If there's little food to be had, best to keep it for night-time. So you can sleep. Worst is going to sleep on an empty stomach. It'll eat its way up you in the night. Sometimes I chewed my braids to make it stop. Stomachs can be tricked if you know how.

Really, Aberfa was orphaned too, poor thing, and saddled with a small sister to boot. But her a married woman—nineteen years old—big enough to have some sense. Different from me. Just senseless as a guinea hen. I was underfoot, but quiet as could be.

Was living in terror of Aberfa dying like Mam and Dat did. For if she went, that'd be me and her little *babanod** all carted off to the orphanage, I was sure. Her man didn't have it in him to tend us all alone. And both her and him without living parents to step in and help. Oh, I lay up awake at night thinking how to keep her alive. And it worked. Later days—when I was nearer grown—I lived in terror, still, of Aberfa dying. But now was the idea of *me* left with all those children of hers. Sometimes she had them two at a time, and they were stacking up.

By nine, knew school didn't suit me. Couldn't abide *something* about it. The penning up, I reckon. No mam or dat to chase me back, I ran wild most days. When the weather was not so bad, hid down the ash groves along Pirate's Path. Eating whinberries, watching clouds. When weather was bad, I went up to Williams's barn and scooted between Williams's two cows there. Was safe in the hours between milkings. Won't say I didn't have some milk most days, fresh from the udder.

Likely my sister was relieved when she knew I'd not been to school. No need to send the school coin for me then. But was unheard of for girls to wander as I did. And yet, no one stopped me knocking loose in the world. Some days I asked Aggie to skive off with me. But she had a real mam to catch her. And a real dat

---

*   Children

to knock her down to next week, need be. So, she kept to school. Though I think she liked school a lot and wasn't interested in missing it. And her dat helped her with her studies 'til she was smart as him, maybe smarter. Aggie always said to me, 'No, Aderwen, no I shan't come away with you, but doesn't mean I'm *not your friend.*'

Well, we met up mornings sitting on the old stone wall runs long Evans's place. Was the wall with all the lichens and little fat plants full of water. A body can eat them as they are, growing right out of the wall. I was slight and small, so it took climbing for me to get up the wall. I dug my toes in, and up I went. And when I got up top, I waited like a pigeon to see Ag skipping round the bend. Up the wall she came for our dinner sharing out. Now, Aggie always had two eggs, and she'd give me one to take. If she had a cut of brown bread, she tore me half that, too. Few times she had pickled onion and bit it in half with her own teeth to give me some. I put it all in my pocket.

Share and share alike, that's what she said. And she meant it. Once she even tried to give me her wool dress she'd growed out of, but her Mam caught wind and said it had to go to Ag's little sister Yo-Yo. Ag had to get it back from me, and it was a shame to both of us. Well, Ag was always badgering me to come to school saying, 'Aderwen, please' with her wrists turned inside out on her big little hips, just like her mam always stood. I always said 'No, not today, Ag.' And she always said, 'I'll only give the egg if you *promise* to come to school *tomorrow.*' Now, I'd say anything for the egg. We both knew it. Just like Mrs. Monroe knew Ag was sharing with me and always put two eggs. I loved the boiled eggs tied up in the lovely red wool bag Ag kept hanging off her belt. Were boiled in their shells, and her mam put a pinch of salt at the bottom of the bag. Was Ag and her eggs keeping me above ground those days. Simple as that. But no one said things so direct back then, God love them.

Nights were home scrubbing and washing with Aberfa. And looking after her man, Gerallt. And babis. 'Til I married the first man was interested. Liked him well enough then, and for good reasons such as his nice eyes, his mule and old cart, and friendly laugh, good as any I'd heard. Aberfa said to me a laughing man is a man with a full belly. And a full belly on him means a full belly on *you*. She said, 'It's no small thing, Aderwen' while she swept the floor.

True, he had a medium holding with geese and pigs, and a good dry barn. Plus, he was being taken on at the quarry. He was sturdy looking, and if you knew how to look, you could see he didn't go to bed hungry. Reckon he might have married a girl who wasn't an orphan, but for some reason or other was me he fancied. Well, I *was* something to look at back then, some folk said. Somehow, I was.

So, I married that laughing man and left Aberfa in the place that was once Mam and Dat's. But I reckon, always it was the landlord's. Aberfa was standing there, her lovely pale face over a steaming pot of cabbage soup. Mam's long spoon in her hand, stirring away, trying to make thin soup thick. Left her man Gerallt behind too, him chipping down the quarry, coming home dusty and tired with strange fevers and coughs. All for granite setts to send away to other lands, to pave England, folk said. Left wailing babis and runny nose tykes, and small children playing acorns on the floors. They waved me goodbye and cwtshed me tight. Every one sweet as the next. Big eyes following me out the door. Food or no, was family, and was mine. And we'd miss each the other fierce. Same time, was one less mouth they had to share with. And they knew it.

Now, you might wonder the name of this husband I took. Won't speak his name. Bile in my mouth still. Makes me twinge to remember our happy courting, our love promises, him touching my hand. Not to mention years of marriage bed, children, supping together. Him telling stories of his day. Us sitting fireside with our clay pipes at the end of day. I believed him true even if he spent some too many nights down one or place or another with his friends. Telling *true stories,* he always said. Was to be expected with a quiet wife like me, and him a talking sort of man, that he'd like the odd night out, he said. And myself, I didn't mind a night alone with the children abed. Night just to breathe and look out the dark window at the cow barn or the pig sty and think of the warm creatures inside. A bit of quiet. We lived happily for a good long time in this way.

BUT ONE EARLY MORNING, just after first light, he came through the door with a babi. And I knew it then. In the split second. Like an arrow in the gullet. There was nothing true about him at all. But still it had to play out.

Tries to give it to me. Newborn scrap barely washed of blood. Rolled in a woolly blanket. Oh, he keeps his face blank as new cheese, and he holds the babi out to me like he's brought me a tea box from Jones's shop any day of the week. But his eyes go up and down the walls. Across ceiling and over floor. Every place there is but my face.

He rolls his eyes at our youngest—thirteen years but home from school with a cold—munching bread at the table. The rolling eyes make the boy take himself outdoors. And now he's holding that babi like he never held one before. Like a glass babi. But he's silent for once. Him who's always talking. Him, the belly-laugher. The teller of true stories. Nothing to say.

So it's up to me.

'Now, what babi's *that?*'

Looks at me, now. Thinking hard.

'Cat got your tongue?' I say, louder than I ever say anything. 'What. Babi. Is. That?'

His mouth moves for a while, like he's trying to cool too-hot stew, before there's a sound.

'Folk say… folk say… Well, Aderwen, they say Jones the Shop once found a babi *dead* on south road. Once way back. Was a sad day that was, sad day indeed. But this is a *lucky* day. See, your man here was quick and saved the life of this little babi. Just in the nick of time, too.'

Plumps out his chest like a squab, making his braces stretch.

'This babi came off the road?' I ask. 'Where off the road, exactly?'

Looks at me. Clears his throat. Asks, '*Ngeneth*,* will we keep this child?'

'Keep this child?' Feel cords throbbing in my neck. Feel words spiking up my throat and there's no stopping them. I'm surprised by all the words I have like watching it all from somewhere else. Surprised by all the energy, too.

'You don't answer me?' I say. 'We will see about *that*. Now. For the last time, *what babi is that?*'

He makes no answer. Lays it in the middle of our kitchen table gently. It closes both murky little eyes. Doesn't mind my shouting and falls to sleep with breakfast's bread plates, crumbs, dirty cups all around. I lean myself against the wall, shutting my eyes. Imagine him and her, whoever she is.

Open my eyes and shout at the top of my lungs, 'Who was the mother of it? She is among us?'

Why won't he just tell me a lie of kindness? Say it was found in a cabbage patch, traded from a gipsy, some such nonsense? I could *make myself* believe a good story, but my foolish man refuses

---

*   Girl (endearment)

to lie. Refuses to tell me the truth and refuses to lie. I could kill him right there.

Open my eyes and see pride in his face. Yes, it's *all over* him. And he *expects* me to take a cuckoo's egg. Expects me to live with no answers. Expects me to swallow it all. Cold hatred opens up my throat like ladles of spring water. Makes my arms rise up to pull our kettle from the hob. Brain him right here.

But no. I sit hard on the kitchen chair. Lift a cup of cold tea from by babi's feet. Gulp it down—smooth and bitter—tea is still tea. And there's babi, little forehead folding dreams. I notice its fine old blanket embroidered with leaves, acorns, squirrels. Soft wool dyed green. No poor mother there.

I cannot bear ill will to an infant. *Will* not. But still I want to dash its brains against our kitchen wall. It means him unfaithful. It means us destroyed. Well, I'm frightened of myself. And neither this babi nor I asked to be set against each other at this kitchen table. I know that much.

Slow as a salted snail, I shove my three dresses, my under-things, my clogs, into my market basket. And my wooden hair-brush full of my own long black hairs. Take my shawl and black hat off the peg by the door. Pull the umbrella from its stand. Why the umbrella? No idea. Not raining. Impossible to know *what* to take away with you when the husband strolls in with a bastard and you've got to go. Umbrella's good as anything else—means a change of weather.

Wish I could cwtsh the children before I leave but none home. Boy sent outside has wandered away. Rest are out to work the quarry, one at school without a cold. Maybe best they can't see me cut so low.

I pull up my spine. Open the door. Walk out, and leave it open behind me. And there's him standing by the table, looking out, surely betting on me having no place to go. Betting on me being back before sunset to live with what he's done.

I MAKE MY WAY further then further. Don't know and don't care where I go. Hoping something strikes me dead so I don't need to wait to die of shame. Stabbing the umbrella in the dirt, leaving a trail of little holes where I go. I think I might throw myself off the cliffs, like Cranstal Jones did, but I'm too angry for it. I think maybe any minute I'll wake up in my bed—only a dream, no horrible husband, no strange babi in my house, no market basket full of clothes dragging down my arm. To find out, I poke down hard on my toe with the umbrella tip. No, no dream. Now I limp along.

He doesn't follow. I can hear that. But I won't look back to make sure, just in case he is. I march straight through town. Try to look neither left nor right, but here's me reflected in shop windows. Is Saturday, so I hope no one is inside watching me. But who knows?

I keep on up-slope, out of town. Past everyone's sheep. Heart beats fast, then slow, then fast. Throat swells wanting tears, but I won't let it begin. Won't be seen crying up the road. Won't be put back to an egg-beggar, is what I think, but still somehow, I find myself in front of Aggie's house. And though we have been only passing friendly for years, now I tap with my umbrella point.

She makes our tea. Fish, cabbages, boiled carrot. Makes me tell her what happened, much as I can stand. She says, 'Tell me what you can.' I tell everything just that once—over fish dinner going cool on its platter.

Was the last time I told it—'til now. Was also the last time Ag cooked. I cooked from then on. Until I couldn't. Thought of my own five children every day. Heartsick for them, I was. But how could I go back home with that babi there? Was like a slap in the face brought to life and howling for bathing and feeding. Was why I never walked back downhill. You think it's just the one day you won't go back to something like that. Think might be that you will handle the next day. Or the next week. But soon you find it's going to be never.

MY OLDEST DAUGHTER, EDNA, back when she was expecting her first, she walked up to Aggie's here one day. Sat near the bean garden with Ag and me, and fiddled fingers against the garden wall where she sat. She talked over everything but that kitchen table babi down below. Never even had to ask her not to bring it up. She already knew not to.

One sunny day—might be two years after Edna was up, maybe three—I spotted pretty young Marged Dafydd passing down below our bean field. Market basket on her hip. Ag was away to market herself, and I was pulling bindweed between bean plants. Was dizzy. Weeding beans sends me cross-eyed every time. But I like freeing beans from weeds.

Young Marged had brown plaits like wet otter pelts. They shined in the sun with her head down, and I could see she was determined to make market early, kicking up dust puffs. She glanced up at me looking down. Caught me broad in the face, then left the path and tromped directly up the slope at me. As the crow flies. I thought to back away and hide inside. But was great effort, her getting to me—coming uphill like a big mare. So, I stayed.

'I'm sworn to secrecy but *won't* have it,' she said getting close. 'I know what poor girl was mother to that babe, and I know what *that one* down below is guilty of, that Twm...'

'No,' I said, 'Don't mention his name.'

She closed her willow market basket and sat on it like was a little stool.

'Fine, I won't then, but is a dastardly deed he's done, that one.'

'The whole village knows it?' I asked.

'No,' she said. 'No one but my old gran and me.'

'Then I won't know it, either.' I sounded strange to my own ear and felt surprised to refuse to know. 'No, thank you. Please don't tell me. I may not be able to bear it.'

I headed for the house, but bean plants tangled over my foot. Sun cut into my eyes. I couldn't see Young Marged making way back down. All of a sudden, I remembered my manners and called down after.

'Care for cuppa tea? Come back up? Come back up?'

But she was already too far gone to hear me. Just as well, I thought. Just as well.

Reckon young Marged Dafydd's visit changed nothing but changed everything. She never came up again. And I'd had my chance.

I grew love for Ag's home, where days passed us smoothly. No frights. No horrid surprises.

My Edna did pass below regular too, and young Marged, and many others. Edna would wave up on market days. She had my own mother's smile as she pitched to market. Wide and pink lipped. But never did she stop.

Ag said I should march right back down if I liked. And if was *her*, she would. 'Take it all back,' she said. You've as much right as any to be in that house, she said. But only if it pleased me. Thing Ag couldn't understand, thing maybe no one but me can understand, is it had nothing to do with wanting or not wanting. Had only to do with could or couldn't. I just *couldn't*. I knew because I tried to go and never was able to get past the bean-garden fence.

LIKE I SAID, WHEN I got very old, just forgot everything. Made me so angry, so angry I broke Aggie's wooden spoons, she says. Cracked them in half one by one—all three—'til she had none at all. I don't remember. Aggie says was no real bother. Says she just stirred with a metal spoon then. She thinks it's a little funny. I don't. I never wanted to be the type of woman breaks people's spoons. 'Specially Aggie's. I do remember, even when I was in my time of spoon-breaking and forgetting, Aggie gave cwtches. And she put my feet up on a stool when they swelled. She put cups of tea in my good hand, the one didn't shake as much.

I'm not supposed to tell, Aggie says, because it's meant to be private. But I think I will anyway because she also says I should say what I mean. And I'm tired of secrets. Here it is: we died in the very same second—the very same place. Was not so long after Ag bought us our new green Aga. I was bathed. Was tucked in—Aggie knows to tuck properly. Was remembering sitting on the lichen wall waiting for my egg. But then I could smell too much anthracite in the stove. But couldn't say so or get up to shut it off. Didn't know how anyway—fancy AGA's beyond me. Ag says she stoked it good. Then she blocked off the flue. On purpose. Says we'd got to *that* point. Says she didn't know it then, didn't know how us dying at the exact same time meant we'd always be together, but it did. And that was a good surprise.

Aggie, have I talked enough, now?

182

The Delight of One's Own Hearth

Yolanda Monroe • 1888-1960

I learned to figure numbers and work the register at Jones's store after Missus left us, and everyone knew I was a good study with numbers though never with letters. I was a handy sort of woman, though never fancy, but I had good red hair with curls that never faded much, not even when I got old. And when I was young, I had strong legs besides that good red hair as well as two dresses of my own. The winter one was wool dyed green and the summer one was calico print, yellow and blue buttoned up the front with cloth buttons. Missus gave them to me when I was hired as we were the same size, nearly. Enough so that the dresses were only a little too long for me and only a little too tight. But I soon let them out and took them up, for I was also handy with the needle and the scissors. You see, Mister had some new dresses for her—to cheer her up—and that's why I could have the old ones.

Anyway, strong as I was then, just sixteen years of age, I could walk for miles and miles fetching this or that from farms or from the shop when Mister forgot something there. And I could make rich stew and bread loaves or sweet pudding with crusty molasses topping. And what's more, I knew to keep tea coming and to shade the crock to keep the water cool for dipping into when the weather was warm. All this I'd taught myself. Once, Mister Jones carried home a round topped crate from one of his trips. It was full of old cooking books from all over the continent. He tried to sell them second-hand at the shop, but most people aren't interested in fancy cooking or new ways of doing things, so he brought them home for me because I had curiosity and intelligence. Now, I'd been to school longer than some, but still I was no good with written words. There's rules about going to school nowadays, but rules or no, some of us have the hardest time learning to read, no matter how many times we had to take the strap to the palm of the hand for failing. Still, I could make some of it out, and there were lots of drawings which showed ways to do things and how foods should look. I *could read*, just very slowly. Sometimes there was flour dust or grease stains on the pages of those books, and I liked that because it made me think of the people who must have been cooking from recipes in my book even years ago. I'm interested in people that way. I just loved to sit in the kitchen corner on the stool any long afternoon when work was done trying to read those cookbooks just like some people might like to read story books. They were full of recipes, which you'd expect, but also full of housekeeping plans. Because there's one right way and a hundred wrong ways to do *anything* in a house. For myself, I wanted to know how to do any little thing right.

When I sat with those cookbooks, I could taste the food right off the page, and sometimes I tried to make dishes from the books, so once in a while, Mister would sometimes read me a page to make sure I understood what was there. And while he read it, I read along. Put it in my memory. But mostly in those days I just looked at them alone and imagined myself a fine lady of my own house—like Missus but better at it all than she was. Perhaps order-ing some girl like me to polish the silver with juice of a lemon and salt, or prepare a rack of good mutton with new potatoes, or even pop quinces between the layers of soft white linens that were surely overflowing from the cupboard I would keep. And if you never smelled a quince getting ripe, you're missing a wondrous smell, I tell you that. Oh, how I daydreamed when I was young and fool-ish. I did more than my share of it, to be certain, as the Joneses didn't ask so very much of me. Less than I'd have been asked at home, really. They left me time to think up all sorts of stories, which was a luxury.

The cookbooks that were not English were mostly French and those had the best drawings ever, so I looked at them a lot—as much as the English ones or maybe even more. He never brought me any in Welsh. He said he'd not come across any in his travels, and why would I want one anyway when I already knew all the Welsh things? That was fair enough. But then he said it wouldn't have mattered anyway, as I wouldn't have been able to read those either, even in my own tongue. Or in English, which was not entirely true, and it didn't need to be said, if you ask me. That was the first time I got angry with Mister, right then.

Most days, the little boy, Siôn, would sit next to me by the hearth, him not taking much room, small as he was. But his braces were always forcing his legs out stiff until he was kicking my shins black and blue. But he didn't mean to bruise me at all. He just couldn't help himself with that kicking. You see, Siôn was always mumbling nonsense sounds and he paid no attention to my cook-books or his stiff leg braces but he liked to be close to me whether warm or cold in the house, and I liked to give him a little cwtsh because he was a good boy and because his mum didn't get up from bed. And besides, I had no one else here to cwtsh. The grown-up Joneses, well they weren't the type of family for much of that, and even Siôn wouldn't cwtsh me back, but he did lean his head on my shoulder.

Now Siôn's thoughts were a mystery to all. Doctor said his brains didn't work right and neither did much of his body, and that was true in some ways, but I believe there was a lot going on in the head of Siôn Jones there. Most of the time he played with wads of clay kept in his pocket, making them into different sized snakes and balls. And while he did it, he was quiet as a carpenter putting together fine pieces of wood would be. You didn't disturb that kind of quiet. Siôn got fresh clay each day from Mister who dug him new bits most mornings from the side of the fern hill— just before he went down the road and through town to open the shop. Mister was like that, kind almost all of the time, but snide as can be on occasion. But even when he was snide, he did it so well you couldn't help but like him still.

Now Missus, she was a beautiful lady with dark hair that she wore piled up on top of her head. She carried her head high and had a neck like a swan—just like one—it could bow low or turn sideways or rise like she was about to flap her wings. It was because of her tall pile of hair and fine neck that Mister used to brag how beautiful she was to everyone in Nefin, and when he did, he always added that she was finer than Dutch plates or French porcelain. The thing is not many people knew about Dutch plates or French porcelain, nor did they care to know, not because they wouldn't think they're pretty but because they don't have use for them. Or for fancy women. The people understand clayware. Clayware won't break so easy, and if you do break it, it's simple enough to get another piece just as nice without any fuss. Mister didn't understand that about them. Not really. And that's strange because he lived here all his life. I reckon there's some things a person cannot see.

I cooked for Cranstal Jones, but she never ate much—mainly just porridge and fruit or some plain root things like carrots or turnips with a knob of butter—or some wild garlic snipped from our back garden. She said to me she was 'far too sad to eat.' And I suppose, considering she kept losing those babis and had a crippled son to worry over, it was right true.

And you know, I might have been her companion in a way if things had been otherwise, because she was no more than a few years older than me. And she had no other friends anyway. But she was in no condition for friends then. Neither did she truly want another woman keeping house and taking over the kitchen—I could tell. You see, Missus had never asked me to come by. No, it was Mister who did, but even so, Missus never asked me to leave either. Most days she didn't say two words to me as she was altogether in her own tormented world. But sometimes I did see her looking at me out of the corner of her eye and then she'd turn away like water over a ledge, and that made me feel most odd.

In time, Mister and I became like parents and Missus became like a tall womanly child who mostly rested in her room and was helpless to remember her own thoughts from one hour to the next. And so, it was Mister asked questions about what was needed at market for the larder. Mister who asked me whether Siôn was well. Or if any post needed to go out. Asked did his waistcoat look too snug.

And Missus let go of her rightful place more and more each time I was asked and she was not. But there's no blame for Mister, because even if he'd put his face right up in hers and put questions to her—even a hundred times—Missus couldn't answer. Not even about the waistcoat. She couldn't speak about such things, though she could have reached out and touched seams on his sleeves if she'd wanted to.

So, who can blame Mister when he moved out of their bedroom and into the smaller one off the kitchen? Because how could anyone sleep with the likes of Missus standing like a ghost at the window all night each night? Staring out like a ghost, she was. I often brought her tea and pulled her away, but she always went back.

Well, of course those people in and around Nefin—especially the Evans cousins with their six fat wagging tongues between them—were always going to around whispering about how Mister had changed rooms only so that he and I could carry on. How *ever* they knew about him changing rooms, I do not know. It might be Evans the Coal saw when he was leaving coal in the kitchen. Whispers of gossip are demon-wisps, my sister Aggie says, and they fly as such. Given a little time, they'll travel from one end of the earth to the other, all the while picking up bits of grit and pig dirt. Aggie doesn't mince words. And that's just what she said, at least when she came at me with the whisper in her own mouth. And I do think it was the Evanses who started it because I know for fact that's who Aggie heard it from. Now, it wasn't just me their tongues wagged over, they had their way with Lili Morgan, Aggie, Aderwen Gethin, pretty much everyone at some point, but I was top of the list and ready for returns.

The main problem was that this gossip about me was the kind that the more you say it isn't so, the more it looks like it is. There's no use protesting beyond a no, then. So, when my sister asked if it was true, my face turned red to near purple and I said, 'No.' And of course, she said I was lying. Now, I wasn't lying, but also, I was. In a way. You see, I couldn't help my face going purple because the truth is I did *want* Mister to have me in his room—and it was something I thought about most days. When I was having daydreams and holding those cooking books. It might be shameful, but there you have it: he didn't, but I'd have let him if he tried. And there's a measure of guilt in that, to be sure.

So, there was Aggie peering at me like she did, her hopping in the dust of the path to the shops like a massive pestered hen, and me—even as she was hopping and I was denying—still, in the face of it all, hoping Mister would creep to me at night. Maybe I was *worse* than if I had been seduced and got it over with. Maybe I was a wanton one. So, I clamped my jaw shut and turned my back on my Aggie. Aggie doesn't go for a back turned on her, and so she didn't even give me a cwtsh before she left me. I watched her stomping down the hill and swinging her big market basket side to side in front.

What happened, you see, was they all made up their own stories about me, including and up to Aggie. And that meant I'd no one in the world to stand up for me. And the village in general hated me because they had decided I was a Jezebel in the flesh. At first, it seemed like they didn't look down on Mister hardly at all, because he was only a man and so he was mostly innocent of what they believed he'd done with me, because he likely couldn't help himself.

Yes, I *did* brush my hair until it shone, hoping he'd notice. Yes, I did pinch my cheeks to make them pinker, all the while thinking meanly how ashen Missus's cheeks were becoming. In for a penny, in for a pound, I reckon. And still, still, still Mister was purely unwilling to notice me in any sort of romantic way. Like he was a stone with legs. So, between him and the village, I had none of the pleasure and all of the pain of a grand affair.

Maybe I shouldn't have told Mister about Missus and rocking cradles by the well nor picnics with Siôn, maybe it was ugly of me. But I did, because I was frightened for the boy—with him so helpless—and frightened for *her* as well. People not in their right minds might be dangerous—to themselves, even—you never can tell. It's just not right having picnics over the graves of babis, is it? But after I told, I did feel I'd wronged her and made a grave mistake because Mister shouted and shouted right up close in her face. It was so bad that I went to shrink away into the corner, and I'm not one to shrink.

Now, when Missus went missing everyone in the village knew she wasn't ever coming back. Well, everyone but Mister that is. Mister just waited for her. Every night, he told me to 'set a place for Cranstal here, because she'll surely be back soon'. But he was wrong. Everyone had looked everywhere for her and found no sign. Mister himself, and me, and all the neighbours—even some in the next villages—they'd rung bells and called out for her. 'Cranstal! Cranstal!' I called out, 'Missus! Missus!' because I just couldn't bring myself to call her by her given name in those days, in case she appeared and thought I'd got above myself. After all, I was only young then. And there I was, along with the rest, beating the grasses and gorse and keeping eyes to the ground for any sign of her. Though I was in love with Mister, I never wished ill on Missus. I never wished for her not to return. In time, after days and days of it, people had to go back to their tasks. And it was called a lost cause. But Mister still looked each day. He even closed his shop for the meantime.

When one shoe and a bit of her best dress washed up on the rocks below the west cliffs, Evans the Pig came to tell him, and fast on that Evans's heels came a wagon driven by Evans the Box, and there in the back, Missus's water-logged body all wrapped in cloth. Well, our Mister was calm as a cow—calm as a cow when a cow is calm—that is. Because when a cow's not calm, it will kill you. His eyes were bulging, and he put his head on the table, but that was all.

In fact, in the next few days, he was so steady that it looked to folk like he barely noticed anything around him. And even much later, even when all of a sudden, his poor crippled Siôn died with an infected splinter, Mister just went on in the same mood because there was no other way for him to feel but sadder than he already was. Maybe when a person has the grief over them so many times, more of it makes little difference. But I could see he still took it in, and he turned inside-out like a person with his skin on the inside and his blood on the out. It was strange that he never left us because Mister could've sold off the shop and bought another somewhere far away from his heartbreak whenever he liked—I'd seen the books and he was right side up in the ledgers, but still he didn't budge.

Now, when Missus had been gone for a decent length of time, I resumed putting myself in his way because I loved him very much even in his grief, and still he only gently moved me aside in a way that reminded me of a person holding their breath to keep from being seen. He kept me on because he was a kind man and I do believe because he knew he'd ruined me, even though he'd never touched me at all. Not even when we were working alone in the shop. Nor when we nailed together a wooden cart for taking curios about for sale. Not even as we got old together. Never once, not even by accident, in all those years that followed Missus throwing herself off the cliff, did he so much as brush my hand nor bump into me—and that's so unlikely to be natural that it makes me know he took great care not to. Obstinate. And some days that made me hateful on the inside.

When I died, I was a creaky old woman in this lovely stone house. And the thing that surprises me still is the house is mine, because Mister left her to me, as well as the shop, when he died. A creaky old man himself, he had no one else to leave to. Neither did I. No one would have me after Missus was gone, them all thinking

I was devious and unrepentant. But I wasn't like Delilah or Jezebel from the Bible. No, those ends are far worse than mine. I did have a good ten years in my very own kitchen as it turned out, with no one to tell me a thing to do. I had time to put quince between the sheets when I could get some down the hill. Time to look at the cookbooks and rattle the pans when I liked. But I was well past daydreaming age, and I'd no guests for dinner except Aggie on the occasion she felt like coming out. And, you know what, that spinster sister of mine, she never stopped digging at me to finally tell her the truth. Even though I'd already told her the truth years before.

I had my favourite cookbook out. Isabella Beeton's one with the linen cover and tiny roses stitched in the corners. I'd memorised the entire thing by then, but I still liked to look. I'd laid it spread open on the table, away from the mess, and set to making cherries in syrup as she said was the best way to do it, with caster sugar. It was a hot day, and the kitchen was steamy with boiled syrup, and by the end of it I stood back to admire how the cherries glistened in glass jars. I listened to the sounds of the jars cooling and sealing tight. Once they were cool, I was planning to queue them up in the cupboard, red as rubies. My joy in cherries and apricots came from the colours and the smells. It was a thing that made me enjoy my own company so much that lots of times I didn't feel alone in the least. But one jar was only half filled and couldn't be sealed like that, so I decided to bake up a simple sponge to go with those cherries and it would be my dinner because there's nothing wrong with a cake for dinner once in a while. But, oh, the kitchen was steaming.

I was thinking about the 'mystery' of poor Lili Morgan—the one person the gossips didn't know about but I did. Lili was a young girl when she was supposed to have gone to London or to her aunt's. Mister Jones always thought she did make it to London.

He hoped it. I could see it in his face, and I hadn't the heart to tell him what was what. The town gossips had sharp eyes, and they noticed she'd been looking as if she might have been in an interesting condition when they saw her in capel. They were sure she'd been sent away to a babi and mother home, never to return. And I didn't tell any of them different because I'm not one to gossip, and I'm certainly not one to give them an inch after how they did to me. What I saw was this: both Marged Dafydds going into the Morgan house late at night, both of them. I was trotting back from the shop with some eggs to boil for me and Mister, who had forgotten to bring any home. We'd thought to go without supper but then decided we couldn't. I'd gone the long way there and back with the key, no short cuts because I didn't like passing the marshy place at night nor the hill of the fair folk. I was moving slow for the likes of me, considering the eggs and not wanting them broken but also keeping an eye out for whatever might come my way in the dark. I was making my way up the road past the Morgan house, when I saw the Dafydds from where I was passing under the willow. I stopped in my tracks. I saw Mrs. Morgan open the door, and I saw the Dafydds hurry inside. Heard the door bolt behind. Now, there are only two possible reasons both midwives will come to the house with their bags loaded as they were. Birth. Or death. *Or both.* And as no one but poor Lili Morgan was missing after that, well, something right devastating went on in that house. I can say that much! Only two possible reasons and both equally terrible for the family if they come at anything other than their appointed time.

I stayed long enough to hear screaming. But there was nothing to do for it. I walked home and made my eggs. I served them to Mister. But I was a bit changed in that I knew a monstrous secret and that I was somehow thankful that despite my predicament, it was not nearly as dire as Lili Morgan's. Now what led up to that, I have no idea. I cannot prove a thing. But a new babi appeared down the hill at the Gethin home, it seems. Some said it was Missus Gethin's and she'd gone up the hill after she'd birthed it. Some said it had come all the way from Pwllheli, found on a big boat there. I kept my mouth shut still. But keeping quiet didn't mean I didn't consider the story. I suppose at the least Lili Morgan had some kind of romance in her life. Even if it had been with Twm Gethin or one of his sons. While I had none.

But then her face was never seen again, and I knew she might well be dead. Dead and the whole thing covered up. Even in my old age, even though she wasn't anyone special to me, I was fairly haunted by her on regular occasion. I suppose it was because she was so young and because I was once young as well, without much of a rudder in life. And then, you should know, that babi went missing, too.

I WAS BENT OVER my fancy, new electric mixer, moving on to other thoughts, when my right arm went dead. Not tingly, just heavy and impossible to move. And my right leg wasn't working well either. I went to lie down, lurching through the place out of the kitchen and down the long hall to my little room which had once Siôn's room, all those years ago, not so long after I arrived here, just a girl then. But I felt so weak that I only made my way as far as Missus's room and barely that—though as a rule I never came in here. I tumbled into her big brass bed hoping to recover, but I drifted away on her blue coverlet looking out her window with my fingers bound together—sticky with cherry juice and sugar syrup.

The Angle of a Sister's Growth

Eirlys Morgan • 1901-1976

I lived my whole life here. In North Wales. In Nefin. Born not long before Cranstal Jones went over the cliff into the sea. It's easy enough to go off a cliff and plunge in. Her and her babies are buried right here which is why I think of them now. It's a beautiful spot and quite abandoned for some long time, except for the quiet burials, like my sister's was. You ask me, there's more than enough to see right here to keep you from looking elsewhere. There's the purple of *Yr Eifl,** the yellow of the gorse, the green-blue-greys of mists and the black of the gales coming in and going out. The surprise of a pale blue sunny day. All sorts of flowers and insects, birds, fish, people. But not too many people. Just enough that you're glad to see them coming your way. Some people call these hills, but I say to myself that they are mountains. The slopes change a little every day—because everything on them changes a lot every day. You'll never look at the same mountain twice. Where

---

*   The Three Rivals, a set of three very large hills or small mountains

you're standing now, six days ago, a load of ladybirds were gathering there. Now they've all scattered to plants hither and yon. You missed them. They come and go. And the branch of that oak, there to your right, only a few days ago the leaves were smaller and paler, hardly stopping the sunlight at all. Now they're giving you real shade.

My mother liked to joke that I was as slow moving as treacle gone cold. She had a way with images, I always thought, and though her saying I moved slowly sometimes made me feel like a strange one, it was no lie. I breathed slowly, walked slowly, talked slowly. I even ate slowly. And I liked being that way. Liked to linger on my way home just looking at things. And that wasn't anything like my sisters Lili and Rhosyn. They were talkative and quick. I often went unnoticed. But I do credit some part of my enjoyment of things to my calm.

If you ask me, nothing good ever came from hurrying about. Just like nothing good ever came to us in North Wales from the east. Only invaders galloping in to take what was ours and convince us we were for it. The worst plague of all. Calling our land their own, carving up our kings, building their fortresses against us. Starving us down to nothing. Silencing the sound of Welsh as much as they could. So why would anyone want to set out in that direction? Now, some say 'you can't change the past so let's make the best of it. The ones living now didn't do the deeds, so we might as well dip into the 'benefits of the kingdom.' But I don't hold with that. Now, my father's people were from the east, but my mother's, they were from here forever. Family being from within and without puts a person in a strange position, but in a good one from which to observe.

It was London put my sister Lili's head in the clouds, made a dolt out of a clever girl. She didn't even have to arrive there—simple *thoughts* of London were enough to destroy her. It was like the English poison, thick and black, spilled all the way over. It grabbed her like a terrier grabs a rat, and shook her senseless till she was addled and went about carrying fashion magazines under her skinny arm and talking like the *Brenhines Y Saeson,** the way she held her mouth. Walking like she had a sceptre in hand and crown on head down the slope to school. And all the while, everyone knew she wouldn't be going anywhere at all. The adults were all counting on time doing its usual work in curing the young of their romantic ideas. Though our mother, not content to wait for time to do its job, tried to cure Lili herself a few times with the sit-down talk. But there was no putting Lils off it, and the thing was, Lili was such a nice girl no one could be harsh enough with her to break her madness. Because that's what it was, madness. So, she went on and on with it and we all let her. Mother, Father, Rhosyn, me, Jones down the shop handing over those magazines to her, the neighbours who smiled at her, all of us. And maybe, I think, we halfway hoped she might make it there to London despite ourselves equally wanting her not to. Oh, I know we did. Foolishness all around.

Now, Lili was lovely to look at, I won't deny that. Nor would I hold it against her. I'm not one to envy. And I'm not—and never was—lovely to look at. Oh, no, don't worry. It's fine. I wasn't horrible either. Just a bit lumpy with hair the colour of nothing much. Eyes a bit watery around the edges. I've got no head for fashion, either, and I don't mind. Though our mother used to say if I put in some effort, it would really go a long way, girl. Only, Lili's beauty didn't do her much good, and if you ask me, it only drew attention from the worst sort of people. Like Twm Geth, that one. Better to leave yourself plain, I say.

---

*   Queen of England

All the other girls—the plain and the lovely the same—knew better than to go anywhere near Twm Geth. You just didn't. Him with his old thing forever pointed at folk—you could see it right through his trousers there. Truth is, boys and girls alike—and grown women too—scattered when he came down the street. Mainly because you didn't want to be seen with him by your friends. And also because he was oily in nature. He'd ask you how you were without ever looking you in the face. But Lili, now, I'm sure she'd been told all about him because we girls all talked about it walking to and from school. But Lils didn't hear half of what was said sometimes, too busy daydreaming. Our mother said she didn't have the sense to come in out of the rain any more. Look now, it's not that I blame her. I just wished she'd had some sense so we might have kept her longer, you know.

And then, it's sad how she hid what happened from me. Hurtful, because I didn't have many secrets, but when I did, I told them all to her. But Lili, she didn't tell me her secret even though I would have kept it. Though I was younger, I'd have had the sense to get her over to the Dafydds for a special cure. I could have helped. But no, she held her secret in until the last moment. If she could have done it, she'd *never* have told, but of course, in a case like hers—with a baby coming—that's impossible. It *will* out. And that it went like it did will always make me sad. She has made me so sad for so long.

I once heard our father say, not too long after Lili died, that she was better off dead after what happened anyway, that she'd never have outlived the shame. And you might think him a monster for saying it, but that's how it was then. He was right. But how I hated him for saying so, because it was also *wrong*. As wrong as right. In fact, I hated him from then on almost as much as I hated that Twm Geth. Oh, he was a terrible one! Riding about in his cart, splashing mud on them at the side of the road like he always had and smiling like nothing was changed. Fairly grinning in our faces. But I knew what had gone on, alright. My sister might have been a flighty one, she might have had her head in the clouds, but she never went looking for Twm Geth. She wasn't a bad girl ever. No, he'd come after her like a whippet after rabbit. And her not even a country rabbit, her one of those soft white rabbits magicians stuff into their hats.

Mother and Father both told us Lili's baby had died within her. Stood there after we'd put her away with long faces. There, in this old graveyard, where no one has been buried since Cranstal Jones and her babis—and before her, no one in memory. Said they were— both of them, then—on top of our grandmother Morgan, who had kindly sunk down enough to make room. The minister had arranged it quietly. No one attended. They said, yes was for the best and we were never to speak of it, but should someone ask after Lili we were to say she'd gone off to care for a sick aunt in Glamorgan and wouldn't be coming back for some time. They said it was all for me and Rhosyn, so as not to ruin our chances. We didn't even know *anyone* in Glamorgan.

But Rhosyn and I were wise to them. We knew it was Lili alone who had gone in on top of our old nain. We knew because we paid attention. Now, we were not allowed out of the loft the long hours poor Lili shrieked there in the sitting room. But we did peer through the crack in the floor down to the sitting room where they'd put Lili on the big bed. What we saw was so terrible we decided not to look anymore. But then when quiet came, we peeked again, and it was then we'd seen the Dafydds– there were two, and I'm talking about the old one now—we'd seen *her* bent up and looking altogether furious while she put the baby in a carrying basket—the one with the blue stripe our mother used for market. And that baby was alive. The young Marged was there, too. Crying and dropping bloodied sheets into a pile. And the tiny baby, it was wrapped in a green blanket the Dafydds had brought with them, mewling with that newborn quiver. Then, out the door went the Dafydds, the baby, the blanket and the sounds. What remained in the room below was our Lili, cold and white and still, bedsheets pulled up to her neck. Balled up cloths all around her. Her hands clasped, ready for the grave. All black under her eyes. Sort of flat looking in the body. We stared through the crack. And there was our mother with stone in her face, staring herself, off into nothing, pulling hairs one by one from her own head. We smelled the stink of blood and tasted it in the air, so strong it was like that. It seeped through the crack at our faces.

For a while Rhosyn and I wondered where the baby had gone to, but then the Gethin boy came up to school, saying there was a new baby down at his place and bragging about how his dat found it right in the middle of the road just last week. He said the baby was smaller than a frog and wrinkled and red-ugly as sin. We knew he was a liar and we made it our business to try to catch a glimpse of it whenever we could, sneaking around the Gethin place, which was not very smart, considering. We knew that little thing was our niece. She was as big as a puppy, and she wasn't ugly at all.

No, I NEVER WENT to London. Like I said, I wouldn't. But Rhosyn, she did. One day she was a child of seventeen in the house with me, and then poof—gone. She most certainly went in the place of our dead sister, Lili. She left a note on the table saying she was done and wouldn't even wait until she turned twenty-one to go off to London and make her way. Mother sat in a chair and pulled at her eyebrows until they were altogether gone. Father shook his fist at nothing and looked at me to be sure I wouldn't go. But that only lasted a moment. He looked away satisfied. We all knew I had no such intentions.

Rhosyn wrote to say she'd found work there in the Big Smoke, as a nanny. Turns out she found it through the post before she even left. She sent me a postcard saying that she went straight to Piccadilly Circus and to the ice rink and to the gardens, even though it was bitterly cold, just to see everything Lili had told us about, to see if it all was true. She said it was true. And that it was lovely in its way, though the people would run you down without so much as a pardon me. And all the people of London wear stone faces outside their homes.

A long time passed, her sending postcards from London, me replying from our tiny post office. Father disowning Rhosyn but still trying to read her letters when he found them. After a time, she met a lovely man—I never saw him though—who worked for the Royal Mail. They married and had a little boy. Rhosyn sent me cards and letters about her street and about the children, signing each Mrs. Rhosyn Lili Sumpter as if she'd carried Lili along with her. My sister Rhosyn, she never set foot in Wales again. And I couldn't force myself to London, so we were, all three sisters separated in the most permanent of ways. But there was love, still. That never left us.

And yet there was injustice—Twm Gethin, that awful man who had ruined Lili, he squawked about free as a magpie with no one but us Morgans the wiser to what he'd done. Though perhaps Yolanda Monroe knew something, for I'd seen her through the window from where Rhosyn and I had been sent that awful night. Saw her lurking under the willow, watching our house. I've always wondered how much she knew, but you wouldn't ever ask a question like that. And us all Morgans shut-mouthed on the subject so as not to bring shame. And then there was Mrs. Gethin—Aderwen Geth, she was called—who stomped up the hill soon after the baby was born and brought into her house—might be she knew what was what. But like me, whatever she thought, she kept her mouth closed. And the midwives kept quiet, too, but that's in the nature of midwives, down to the bone.

Her name was Betsan, Lili's child, and when I became a schoolteacher's helper. I made sure to fix it so that the child was under my eye. She was delicate like Lili had been but darker of hair and taller, with the Gethin self-assuredness about her. She had some trouble making her letters at first—pulling her pencil bottom to top instead of top to bottom, which got her punishment. But she was a clever little girl who spoke like a grown up, bright as a button. I helped her with the pencil until she had a lovely hand.

I watched Betsan carefully for any sign of trouble, for any clue that the wicked old man who called himself her 'adoptive father' had been at her. I wouldn't put it past him. Where does a man like that draw the line? The thought wriggled like a worm in my ribs, so I confided in Mother. At first, she didn't want to hear it. But I cornered her while she made jam one week, describing the child until she finally cried and cried over the steaming strawberry pots. You see, Father had died earlier that year and Mother had changed.

With Father gone, we hadn't much money, but we managed to hatch a scheme. I saved my helper's wage for nearly three months to purchase two tickets out of Pwllheli by steamer to London, second class. I helped my mother mend her best dress, and we found some sturdy traveling shoes for her at the shop. I put extra money in a small wallet for Mother—for clothes for Betsan, to be purchased later. To be plain about it, you see, Mother and I *kidnapped* Betsan. Just as she walked to school on the second of December, 1924, we took her. We told the poor thing that she'd won a very important prize in London, that there was a lovely school for her to attend that her father had said we were to get her to as soon as possible. We said there was only one place open, and some other girl might take it. In fact, there were so many other girls who wanted to go, that we'd have to hide her under blankets so that those girls didn't catch a glimpse and try to get there ahead of us. Betsan tilted her head for a moment, like a robin listening for worms, and then she nodded and slipped her little hand into that of the grandmother she'd never met. And that's how my mother went away with Betsan. I drove them in the back of my father's rig, hidden under blankets to Pwllheli where no one would know them. They sailed for London, where Rhosyn waited to take our dead sister's daughter into her own home, as her own.

Mother stayed for some time to visit and to see the sights there in London. And perhaps she'd have liked to remain, but she did not. After Mother returned, Rhosyn wrote that Betsan was adjusting quickly and was loved greatly there in London, but she referred to our girl as 'the pup' in all her letters, just in case there was any steaming of envelopes in the post office. I cannot even begin to imagine the lies Rhosyn must have had to spin to the child to make her happy. Betsan, like Rhosyn, would never return to Wales. Not in my lifetime.

Oh, but how Twm Gethin did the work when the girl went missing. Played the victim like he was after an award. Even I almost felt sorry for him once or twice. But no one had seen anything, and Gethin chalked it up to gipsies in the end, I heard. I made it my business to grin at him every chance I got from that day in 1924 until his death in '42. I can only hope he understood somewhere in the pit of his stomach. He might have suspected us, but he could never have accused us without the dirty truth coming out for all to know. What he did to my sister. Serves him right.

You see, every week from the time I was a young woman, I've come on my own up to the graveyard to visit the stone-less grave of our Lili, thrown in secret atop the old nain, no thought to her dignity, to her memory. I often wished Gethin was buried in the same place, too, so I could trample his bones properly and regularly as it's quite private here. As with most bad men, he lived a long time, so I had to wait. But I outlasted him by some long time, and when he *was* finally buried, in the graveyard down, where the new capel is, with a proper stone and all—well, I made sure to walk across him there. He was pulverised by a propeller plane, can you believe it? There was not much beyond a few fingers and ashes, is what I heard. The winkle picker saw it all happen. And I'm sure the soul of him is still there on the strand, where he drew last breath. You might think I'd have plenty of company here in the cemetery, but as I'm the only one who drew last breath here, I'm completely alone. Just bones are here. I know that much. Mother and Father's are over in the proper graveyard with Gethin, and so, I suppose, are my own bones by now.

When I came here to Lili's grave as an adult, I liked to bring up the cards and letters from Betsan. I read them to Lili because I knew Lili would be interested in the fashions and the news from London. You don't know if a person can hear what you say at their grave, and you think they are where they were buried instead of where they lived. You decide you might as well give it a try. You do your best, you see with whatever it is you think you might know.

I was never sure how Rhosyn explained the details to Betsan as she got older. She must have found a way, she must have done it bit by bit. She did her best, too. As did Betsan, who's an old woman herself now. As we all do.

Me, I never married. Never had a family of my own. I just never got around to it. I helped at the school till I was old. I volunteered at the hospital in the evenings, doing colouring and yarn crafts with the children there and any adults well enough and friendly enough. On weekends I worked in the cat's charity card shop down in the next village. I got a little bit of aid here and there. Rented half a cottage down at the bottom of all the hills.

I had my own car, too. But the big event was never mine; it was always Lili's and I just lived in the wake of her somehow. Outside of the day we kidnapped Betsan, my life came in like waves, with few changes much made by me. Some days, I thought of myself as much like the pink jellyfish that float in each spring down at the cove. Jellyfish go nowhere on their own, but aren't they just as alive as the other ocean and sea things? Don't they enjoy floating about? Don't they have the calm to observe? And then sting when the time is right.

I was old enough that I'd sore knees and hips by the time I died here. Rhosyn was gone herself a few weeks past, and I'd just finished reading a letter aloud to Lili in her grave about it, the one Betsan sent about poor Rhosyn. An inveterate smoker, she was. Inside was a photo of them all sitting in a café—from before the cancer. Rhosyn looked like our mother, with a long face and the straight thick hair. With round grey eyes. I tried to imagine what Lili might have looked like if she hadn't gone so soon, but she'd been gone so long by then that I could barely remember her young face anymore. Not clear and sharp anyway. Best I could do was remember her silhouette, head to toe, and her walking head-down with the sun on her side, tripping up the old road back home with her sack of cut-outs swinging from her hand. I patted the green over her grave like I was patting her slender little arm, for she'd always be young to me though she was my older sister.

That day, ladybirds, hundreds of them crowded over a stone in the sun a little way over from me, all red and black with their perfect spots. All trying to catch the sun. The graveyard was full of chirp and light, and I was warm in my old purple woolly jumper. Down on the ground I leaned up against an unreadable old stone from another time, the letters and numbers, like so many, worn down to just a few lines you might feel with your thumbnail. And lichen clogging those remaining lines as best it could. There's always a cool wind up high here, though, and I pulled the jumper up to my nose. Still had car keys in my pocket and my reading glasses on the top of my head when I dozed off and never woke up again. Not in the old way anyway. No matter, I'm still here. At home in Nefin, watching slopes change. Watching the sea, too. Listening for the curlew and whoever may pass by.

Christina Marrocco is an award winning author from the Chicago area. Her 2022 debut novel, *Addio, Love Monster* won the Book of the Year award from the Chicago Writers Association. Her doctoral dissertation, *The Evil Eye in Italian American Literature* established her reputation in ethnic studies. She's also a poet whose work has appeared in many journals including *Ovunque Siamo*, *The Laurel Review*, *Silverbirch Press*, *House Mountain Review*, *Red Fern Press*, and *Voices from the Attic*. Christina teaches Creative Writing and other courses at Elgin Community College. Further information on Christina's books, events, workshops, book club visits and more can be found at ChristinaMarrocco.com.